THE
ADVENTURES
OF
THE COWL

ANTHONY GIANGREGORIO

IN THE CLUTCHES OF
THE PUPPET MASTER

The Cowl brooded in his lair, his eyes scanning the files on the massive computer screen before him.

There had been a rash of bank robberies lately, and though hard to believe, the eyewitnesses stated the robbers were zombies.

One security guard had even managed to get off a shot into one of the backs of the robbers, and the robber had taken the shot without flinching.

At first, the police assumed that the man was wearing body armor, but later, as the investigators studied the crime scene, bits of flesh and bone were found splattered on the wall, exactly where the guard had shot the robber. The guard swore up and down his shot was directly over the robber's heart, but if that was so, and the bullet had connected with the robber's heart, then what other explanation was there as to why the robber remained standing?

Above his head, bats slept, the massive cave of his lair was like a giant tomb, hiding him and all of his secrets. Above the lair was his mansion, where he played the lay-about playboy, but his true personality, the heart of *him*, was revealed when he was the Cowl.

After a tragic carjacking when he was a boy, the Cowl found himself an orphan. Inheriting a large corporation, he soon found ways to channel the rage he had bottled up from the unfair and tragic death of his parents.

Now, he prowled the streets of the city, searching for evil wherever it might rear its ugly head.

The police scanner began to crackle static and the dispatcher called out an all points bulletin. There was a robbery being reported at the First City Bank, and the robbers were there at that exact moment.

Without a second to waste, he slid his leather mask down to cover his face, jumped from his chair, and dashed across the lair. His car was waiting, a large, black, armored sedan, tricked out with more gadgets than anyone could imagine.

The top slid open as he approached and he jumped into the driver's seat. With a blast of fire from the powerful engine—which used jet fuel—he tore out of the lair and down the long winding tunnel that would take him to an exit a half mile from the closest main road.

It had cost millions to make the tunnels and the lair itself, and he'd made sure to do it in piecework to prevent each contractor from knowing what each tunnel was for. Few had asked questions, after all, the whims of the rich are many and extreme. Who would ever understand their crazy projects? But when secrecy wasn't a guarantee, legal forms and money had done the rest, ensuring the security he needed.

The black sedan cut through the dark streets like a scythe, the headlights slicing the cold winter night. The First City Bank was on the north side of town and it was the tail end of rush hour.

He used his extensive knowledge of the city to avoid any traffic snarls, and with a little bit of luck thrown in for unexpected obstacles, he still pulled up in front of the bank within ten minutes of the call.

Jumping out of the car, he ran up the stairs, taking them three at a time; his black cape flowed behind him, fluttering in the wind.

Pulling the far right glass door open, he entered the bank warily, but no sooner did he enter, then a piercing scream rent the air and bullets began to fly, peppering the glass doors behind him.

One door shattered, spraying glass shards onto his back, only his cowl and cape protecting him from serious harm. He rolled across the marble floor and hid behind a large stone desk. He felt his left arm pulse with pain and noticed he'd been hit by a stray round. Checking the wound with his glove-encased fingers, he noted also, that it wasn't serious.

Poking his head around the side of the stone desk, he took in his surroundings in a glance; he had a full view of the lobby of the bank, and the tellers and customers, too.

All the customers were on the floor, and two security guards were lying dead on the floor, pools of blood surrounding their still bodies. It looked like one guard had his throat torn out, but the Cowl wasn't close enough to know for sure. It seemed the robbers had escalated to murder as well as armed robbery.

Three of the robbers were standing in the center of the lobby, each holding a gun—AKs by the looks of them—guarding the customers, and three more were shoveling money into cloth sacks.

From the Cowl's vantage point, he couldn't get a good look at the robbers' faces, but it appeared they were wearing rubber masks of some kind, which would explain the descriptions that had come in about zombies.

Panicked and terrorized customers, plus rubber masks of zombie faces, would make even the most rational person believe the impossible. Perhaps the security guard who said he shot a robber in the heart was wrong and the bullet hadn't killed the man, or he'd died later after escaping.

All thoughts of 'what ifs' went out the door when a teller screamed as a robber attacked her for no reason.

The Cowl wanted to help her, but because of the robbers' heavy firepower he knew he needed to come up with some kind of plan first.

But all thoughts of plans went out the window when the robber did something The Cowl couldn't believe, even though he saw it with his own eyes.

The robber pushed the bank teller—a woman in her thirties—across the counter and leaned over her so his teeth were touching her neck; he sank them in, tearing her throat out with a yank of his head.

Blood shot forth as the bank erupted into chaos. The robbers' AKs were the only things keeping people from simply jumping up and running away. With whimpering and screams for mercy filling the lobby, the robber fed on the teller like a lion would a downed gazelle.

Over the din, the crunching sound of the robber feeding filled the air, making the customers who could see it vomit on the floor. This caused others to do the same, and soon there was a massive barf fest occurring, mixed in with cries and pleas for help.

One of the robbers turned and started walking towards the slain teller, perhaps to get a piece himself, but slipped in a pool of throw-up. As his foot landed on bits of hotdog, French fries, and a half-digested salad, his foot went out from under him as if he'd stepped on ice. He fell onto his back and his gun went off, his finger squeezing the trigger on instinct. The overhead fluorescent lights and the skylights shattered, bits of tiles and glass raining down, and for a moment, caused even more pandemonium.

The Cowl used this distraction to go into action.

He stood and spun on his heals while grabbing three Cowlarangs from his utility belt; he flung them through the air before anyone even spotted him, hitting the two remaining guards—one in the eye and the other in the neck. Moments after their sharp edges embedded in the robbers, they exploded, spraying the bank and customers with brain matter and blood, before the beheaded robbers flopped to the floor like a dead fish.

The third 'rang flew beyond the robbers guarding the retching customers to ricochet off of a steel support beam, standing between the bank teller area and the loan officers' desks—right over the head of the robber snacking on the woman. It exploded, sending sharp shards of metal through the air in all directions, one entering the back of the eating robber's head; he groaned weakly and dropped to the floor.

Metal shards shredded the face of the robber who'd slipped and fallen; he was pulling himself up on the counter, eager to join his comrade in the feast. The injuries didn't slow him down at all. His head had tilted back slightly at first impact, but otherwise it didn't even faze him; he continued where his buddy had left off.

The other two robbers close to the counter dropped their bags of cash and turned towards the Cowl, opening fire. He spun sharply, causing his cape to billow out and around him, making him a larger target. Multiple bullets zipped through the fabric, but none came close to hitting him. His trained hands extracted a small vile from another compartment of his utility belt, and as he faced the robbers again, he paused and threw it at their feet, before dropping and rolling closer to the counter. The contents of the vile exploded as it hit the floor, sending up a billowing cloud of dark purple smoke laced with tear gas. The customers screamed and groaned in agony as they tried to scoot away, blinded by the gas; it didn't effect the robbers at all. They grinned, picked up the cash, and opened fire again without aiming as they charged for the main doors.

The Cowl stood and took a couple of steps to them, but the sound of police sirens halted him; he couldn't be seen by the local law enforcement as he was on their most wanted list. It didn't matter that he'd help keep the citizens of the city safe, he was a vigilante and that was illegal, too. Thinking quickly, he withdrew a small gun from a holster on his hip. He raised his arm and pulled the trigger, sending a small grappling hook up and through one of the broken skylights, giving it a quick tug to make sure it was anchored. He pushed a small button on the handle of the gun and was drawn upward; while in motion, he withdrew a small tracking device that looked like a barbed ball—about the size of a tiny gumball—and threw it at the departing robbers, hitting one in the back just as he stepped through the door. It stuck.

Smiling broadly, knowing he'd be able to track the ones who got away, the Cowl departed the bank through the hole in the roof and was out of sight as the first responding police officer came through the main doors of the bank. Yelling loudly, the first officer ordered the robber attacking the woman to cease and put his hands up, but the zombie robber didn't answer and kept on eating. Two loud shots rang out and the Cowl knew the last of the robbers within the bank had been taken down.

Staying low and out of sight on the roof, the Cowl watched the police scramble around the building, barricading and forming road blocks below. To him they looked like ants that didn't know what to do, but were working hard at it nonetheless.

Flipping open the top of his watch, he pushed a small red button and smiled when he heard his vehicle below roar to life. Unlatching a little stick below the button, he guided his car out of an alley and around the corner, through one of the road blocks, trying not to laugh hysterically at the ignorant police who jumped out of the way and hollered in surprise. Other police officers, who weren't in the way of the car, shot at the tires, trying to deflate them and prevent the vehicle from escaping; the bullets bounced off with no effect, ricocheting back at them while they ducked for cover; even the tires were bulletproof. Using the small arrow keys beside the red button, he set the car to drive for three blocks, knowing it would come to a stop on its own after the programmed distance.

With a sigh and a quick check of his injured arm, he set off, jumping off and gliding from rooftop to rooftop to where his car would stop, knowing he was getting closer with each step to catching whoever was behind the zombies and their string of bank robberies.

Sitting in his lair, the Cowl studied the map on the computer screen in front of him where a small red light blinked in the center of the warehouse district. His arm was bandaged and his Kevlar battle suit repaired, and he was almost ready to leave to finish the mission.

After some quick research, he'd found that the warehouse the robbers retreated to was owned by a dummy corporation, but the trail had gone cold once it led overseas.

Whoever owned the warehouse had money, there was no doubt about it. After the robberies, he knew the money wasn't gained lawfully.

After restocking his utility belt and having a quick bite to eat, he walked across the lair. This time he passed by his car and continued down a long hallway. Eventually the hallway ended and he climbed a flight of steel stairs, his heavy combat boots echoing with each step he took. At the top of the upper landing was a reinforced metal door. He pressed his thumb to the print-reader on the side of the door and the latch clicked, the door popping open with a faint hiss.

Entering, he looked on his pride and joy, a slight smile creasing his lips.

His jet plane sat before him, painted black with sleek lines and an engine that could break Mach 1.

The entire hangar was built under the land he owned, the exit built into the side of a cliff, a massive sliding door hiding the opening was camouflaged with trees and rocks. Even when the door was open, from the ground it was difficult to see unless the viewer knew exactly where to look; the exit was recessed back into the cliff side so that the natural rock of the cliff barrier prevented discovery.

He needed stealth on this part of the mission, and with the police on full alert after his car escaped the barricade, he knew he'd have to take to the sky to remain undetected.

Minutes later, he finished his preflight check and was soaring through the tunnel and into the night sky. Adrenalin filled his system as he flew over the treetops with the city's skyline only a few miles away.

When he reached the city, he stayed below radar detection, flying close to the rooftops. Banking west, he aimed the nose of the jet toward the waterfront.

He was there in minutes. Setting the autopilot so the plane would circle the area, he pressed a button on the joystick and the canopy began to retract. As the jet slowed to stalling speed, he punched out when he was over the warehouse he knew the robbers were in.

Even with his full body suit and oxygen mask on, he could feel the brittle cold slap his exposed flesh. His cape flapped in the wind until he flexed it just so, causing the membrane lining it to snap into position. Using the cape like a hang glider, he began his spiraling descent to the buildings below.

Checking his wristwatch, he noted the round orb now had a small red dot blinking just off center, indicating the tracker was working and that he was in the right place.

It took mere minutes to reach the warehouse, and as he retracted the membrane, allowing the cape to become flexible again, he tucked into a ball when he was twenty feet above the roof and came in harder than he would have liked. He rolled for more than thirty feet on the gravel covered tar, knowing his speed could easy break a limb, and he only spread himself out when he knew he was about to go off the edge of the roof. He calculated almost perfectly, but it still wasn't exact, and as he opened his body, he found he was only mere feet from the edge.

As he slid off the roof, his hands reached out and he managed to grab the edge. Even with his thick leather gloves, the metal lip of the edge bit deep into his palms.

His legs flew over the side to stop with a jerk in midair and come back down, his entire body slapping the side of the building heavily; he hung by his fingertips, his body vertical.

Though the wind had been knocked out of him, he slowly began to pull himself up, his mouth set in a tight grimace. Only his indomitable will kept him from falling, and a lesser man would have let go and tumbled to a painful death on the hard ground below.

As he pulled himself over the edge, he let himself take a moment to rest, sucking in air as his heart beat in his temples.

For a full minute he did nothing but breathe, sucking in great lungfuls of air to suffuse his body with oxygen. But he couldn't stay like that all night, he had a job to do.

Rolling to his knees, he scanned the rooftop for signs of movement. When he found none, he rose and walked until he found a skylight. It was dirty and he had to rub one of the glass panes with his glove to allow him to see into the building below.

Using a pair of night goggles taken from his utility belt, he peered into the warehouse, and his mouth fell open at what he saw.

If he wasn't seeing it with his own eyes, he never would have believed it. Below, more than a hundred people stood together in the center of what seemed to be a massive room. From what he could see, it looked like it was some kind of meat packing factory.

There were long, stainless steel tables surrounding the crowd on all sides, looking as if they had been pushed out from the center; there were even large gouges in the floor where the tables were dragged carelessly. On all sides of the group, the tables were still in neat rows, and he could tell the area in the middle had been cleared…but for what purpose?

As he studied the crowd, he saw each one wore the same kind of mask the bank robbers had worn.

He sat perfectly still, his dark outfit making him just another shadow. While he was watching the crowd, a section shifted and he saw what was obviously a mangled body; it reminded him of the teller back at the bank. More than a dozen of the 'people' were feeding on the corpse, tearing parts away like they were wild animals. As he scanned the rest of the crowd, he witnessed similar groups huddled over what he could only assume were more bodies.

He zoomed in on some of the faces of the crowd, and as he did, he gasped in shock. They weren't wearing rubber masks as he'd once thought; there was no question about it.

Those faces were real, with gaunt expressions, slack-eyed stares, some with mortal wounds and skin the color of dried parchment.

The rumors of the dead robbing banks was true, and worse still, there was an entire army of them hidden inside the warehouse.

But who was keeping them? Who was pulling all the strings? Who was the criminal mastermind?

It was while he was running through names of his villainous foes in his head that he picked up on gravel crunching beneath a pair of shoes.

Someone was behind him!

Pulling his eyes away from the carnage below, he spun around in time to see one of the dead coming at him. Its arms were out, making it look like a Frankenstein imitator, and the Cowl hesitated for the briefest of moments, not sure what to do. He didn't know if he should kill it or leave to come back with reinforcements after being discovered.

But the decision was taken from him as the zombie charged straight at him, wrapping its arms around him and sending the Cowl falling backwards, right into the skylight.

With the sound of crashing glass and air rushing by him once more, the Cowl found himself falling again, and all the while the zombie was trying to sink its teeth into his exposed neck, ignoring the fate, it too, would share when they landed on the cement floor below.

Twisting and forcing his body mass to the side, he reached for his gun, drawing it from the holster at his hip and raising it the best he could while in a bear hug of death with the zombie. He pulled the trigger and the grappling hook whizzed through the air to loop through one of the steel beams supporting the ceiling, the three prong tip catching as the wire began to slide. With a sudden jerk, he came to a stop when his weight, and that of the zombie, met the end of the wire connected to the grapple; the zombie had just leaned in for another chance at the Cowl's artery when the jerk loosened its hold and it continued falling while the zombie's meal remained suspended in the air.

Moaning and pawing at nothing, the zombie dropped into the center of the crowd of undead below; landing on three of its decomposing partners, causing a messy splatter of guts, blood, and intestines. The gore coated those zombies standing close by, and they grunted and turned their heads back and forth, confused as to where the falling body had come from.

One of the dead finally looked up and spotted the Cowl only a few feet away; it groaned its find to the others and soon the entire crowd was looking up.

The Cowl knew he'd been spotted when all the zombies began groaning, moaning, and clawing at his feet, which were only a yard from their grasping hands. Swinging and kicking, he tried desperately to stay out of their grasp. He pushed the button on his gun to try and go upward, but remained where he was.

Silently cursing, he saw that part of his gun had been damaged by the excess weight of having to hold two bodies and the sudden stop a moment ago; it would hold him aloft, but it wouldn't move him.

With frantic eyes, he looked around for a way to escape. There was a four-foot thick scaffolding that went from one side of the building to the other, and as his gaze fell upon it, he saw his arch foe appear.

The Puppet Master stood tall in a dimly lit doorway, with his arms crossed and a twisted grin on his partially, mask-covered face. The dark green and reflective gold of his disguise added a festive air to his otherwise demure demeanor. Cold blue eyes seemed to glow with malice as he watched the Cowl swing above his undead minions. He cackled an evil laugh, shook his head, and walked deeper onto the scaffold, admiring the predicament the Cowl was in.

"They're hungry, you know," the Puppet Master taunted. "One slip and it'll be the end of you, or maybe I can help you along a bit." Smiling again, he focused on one of the zombies. It froze for a moment, like its mind had gone completely blank and was being reprogrammed. With a flinch and a grunt, it came back to itself and marched straight over to one of the tables and started to climb up onto it and closer to the Cowl.

The zombie soon stood on the table and began clawing at the Cowl's cape, pulling him closer and closer.

"You see, I can control them," the Puppet Master said, watching with glee. "It's amazing what the power of suggestion can do to a weaker mind, isn't it?" He laughed again, throwing his head back in true, sadistic merriment. "The dead have very weak minds and are just lying around everywhere. I dug them up, and I gave them life again. Now they serve me and do my bidding, keeping me in funds. And they never ask any questions or want anything for themselves, well, other than a fresh meal from time to time, and I'm more than happy to oblige."

The Cowl kicked violently, trying to tear his cape free from the clawed hands of the zombie seeking his flesh.

"You won't get...away with this," the Cowl gasped, trying to concentrate on the zombie and breaking free of its grasp.

"Yes, I think I will," the Puppet Master said. "I have slaves that will do anything I want and who can't be killed. Who's going to stop me?"

To prove his point, he raised his arms with his hands flat, palms facing down; four more of the zombies went still and then snapped to attention, heading for the tables to climb higher as well.

"As long as they're fed, they're easy to control, over-willing to please even," the Puppet Master bragged. "Soon, I'll control the entire city and there's nothing you'll be able to do about it, because you'll be dead, providing meat for my army of the dead!"

"You'll never rule this city," the Cowl growled, then kicked out at two zombies on the same table, as more joined the one who was wrestling with his cape. "Not as long as I'm alive."

The Puppet Master laughed. "Poor choice of words, Cowl. You'll be dead in a few minutes." He pointed to the rafters where the grappling hook was holding the superhero suspended above the undead crowd.

The Cowl's eyes followed the Puppet Master's gesture to see a zombie crawling along the steel beam his grappling hook was attached to, a knife clenched between its yellow teeth; it didn't even notice that the blade was cutting into its cheeks and dripped dark blood down on its friends. In moments, the zombie reached its target and started sawing at the thin wire with the serrated side of the knife.

"You won't get away with this, Puppet Master," the Cowl growled, still kicking and twisting in mid-air, barely keeping himself free of the hands eagerly grabbing for him.

Suddenly the wire snapped and the Cowl began to fall into the midst of the hungry horde of zombies. He twisted in the air and came down on the shoulders of an old woman. He flattened the old crone to the floor, the body cushioning his fall.

Some of the zombies staggered backwards with the force of contact as he bumped into them, and some of them fell over to flail uncontrollably on the floor. Jumping to his feet, he withdrew an eight inch knife from a sheath attached to his thigh. He spun and slashed at the bodies around him, his training the only thing saving him from sudden death.

Bloated stomachs burst and slick, rotting innards fell to the concrete floor with a sickening *plop*. The stench of decay filled the warehouse, causing both the Cowl and the Puppet Master to gag.

"Well, I never said they were the most aromatic of minions," the Puppet Master joked.

Stepping forward and stabbing violently, the Cowl advanced through the confused crowd of zombies toward the far wall, seeing a chance to escape the undead mob. But he needed to make it out of the press of dead bodies, organs, and severed body parts first, he just didn't know if it was possible. He was still just a man, trying to right the wrongs of the world, and he began to wonder if he had what it took to save the city this time.

Out of the corner of his eye, the Cowl spotted a row of nitrogen tanks sitting in the far corner of the room, about thirty yards away. An idea bloomed in his overworked mind and he knew what he could do to get out of this mess, or at least stop the Puppet Master and his minions, even if it took his life as well.

With renewed vigor, he slashed and cut, severing heads with his violent swings, slicing through rotten flesh as if the zombies were made of paper mache.

They came at him one at a time, each blocking the rest from attacking in force, and that was his saving grace. If they had attacked en masse, he never would have been able to stop them from swarming him, but as it was, he managed to hold his own until he reached the far wall.

With a drop kick to the closest zombie, he jumped up and grabbed hold of a light fixture with his right hand, then pulled himself up, his other hand grasping on to an electrical box with three fingers, as he still held the knife. After pulling himself up some more with his right hand, he sheathed the gore-covered knife and began to climb faster. The wall had many protuberances and it was child's play for him to scale it like a ladder.

"Get after him, you fools!" the Puppet Master screamed at the zombies, who began to climb, their master's control allowing them the dexterity to scale the wall almost as swiftly as the Cowl. Though controlled by their master, some still were too withered from the grave to climb and their hands slipped, their bodies tumbling back to the floor to splatter like overripe melons.

But for every one that fell, two more continued to climb.

When the Cowl ran out of things to grab, he found himself trapped yet again.

His eyes searching for an escape route, he spotted a hanging electrical wire dangling from the ceiling ten feet away. At one time a light fixture had been attached, but when it had been removed, some lazy worker had merely cut the wire to let it dangle. With the first zombie reaching up to grab his leg and pull him off the wall, he did the only thing open to him. He jumped and grabbed the hanging electrical wire, thus escaping the trailing zombies.

"Very clever, caped crusader, but not clever enough," the Puppet Master said angrily. "I guess I'll just have to finish you off the old fashioned way." With a snarl of rage he pulled a gun from his jacket and aimed it at the Cowl.

Knowing he had seconds to act, the Cowl pulled his last Cowlarang from his utility belt and armed it, the small explosive charge in the tip filled with C-4. As the light began to blink, he swung himself around so he was facing the nitrogen tanks, then threw the 'rang as hard as he could.

As he let it fly, he began to climb the electrical wire, bullets already ringing out around him. One clipped his left leg, causing him to grunt in pain, but still he climbed.

The explosive Cowlarang landed in the middle of the tanks, and though it didn't penetrate the thick canister it hit, it did bounce off to fall at the base of them. Seconds later, the charge went off, rupturing more than half the tanks, the ensuing explosions tearing apart the rest.

Nitrogen gas began to flood the warehouse and a thick cloud rushed across the floor, swallowing the zombies whole. The Cowl managed to just climb high enough to avoid the frost cloud but even so, his feet became cold as they dangled within inches of the mist.

On the scaffolding, the Puppet Master was knocked over from the blast, shrapnel from the canisters peppering him, causing him to drop down and shield his face. The zombies on the wall were knocked off and were soon lost from sight in the white cloud.

The Cowl hung over the white mist, waiting to see what would happen next, and as each second passed, slowly, the cloud began to dissipate.

As he hung there, he looked down on eighty plus statues, all frozen solid from the gas.

A gunshot pulled him from his stupor and another round sliced across his upper shoulder, causing him to grunt in pain. Turning, the Cowl saw the Puppet Master was up and trying to shoot him again.

Swinging his legs, the Cowl began moving back and forth, much like a trapeze artist. Soon, he was swinging wide, and with one final swing, he let go of the wire, flipped in the air, and came down on the scaffolding on bent knees, his weight causing the entire structure to shake for a moment.

"Curse you, Cowl, you've ruined everything. I'll see you in Hell for this," the Puppet Master hissed as he shot his gun at point blank range. It only clicked on an empty round.

"You should have kept better count, Puppet Master," the Cowl hissed then ducked as his enemy threw the useless gun at him. It bounced off the railing to his side and fell to the floor below, landing on a zombie's head. The head shattered into a hundred pieces, leaving the frozen statue decapitated.

"I'll kill you!" the Puppet Master screamed and charged the Cowl. The lower half of his face that wasn't hidden behind his mask was filled with rage at the Cowl's interference.

The Cowl simply sidestepped him and used the villain's momentum to push him away, but as the Puppet Master went flying past the Cowl, he lost his footing and ended up falling over the waist-high railing. As his body flipped over, his hands desperately reached out, grabbing the railing on its lowest rung—one of three—his legs dangling down.

The Cowl spun around and leaned over the railing, trying to grab the Puppet Master's hands. "Here, reach up to me. Give me your hand!" the Cowl yelled.

The Puppet master began to laugh as his fingers started to slip "You'd like that wouldn't you? To save me and take me to jail? Well, I won't give you the satisfaction. Let it be on your head, Cowl, you killed me!" He let go, laughing as he plummeted the twenty feet to the floor below.

The Cowl could only watch as the Puppet Master fell away, as if in slow motion, his body landing on three of the frozen zombies. The way the bodies shattered under the Puppet Master's weight, one ended up having a large shard as sharp as a spear.

The Puppet Master's laugh ceased abruptly as he was impaled on the frozen shard; it went straight through his sternum. Spitting blood, he gazed up at the Cowl. Even in his last moments on Earth, he taunted the caped crusader. As his head slumped to the side and the master joined his minions in oblivion, the Cowl looked on with a stoic face.

"You reap what you sow, Puppet Master. I feel no guilt for your death," he whispered as he stared at his fallen foe.

Police sirens could be heard in the distance and the Cowl knew it was time to leave. Some security guard in another building must have called the police after hearing the explosion.

He needed to get to the roof but he didn't have his grappling gun. He would have to take the normal way, meaning the stairs.

Turning, he dashed down the scaffolding and into the section of the warehouse set up for offices. It only took him a minute to find the stairwell leading to the roof and he ascended it, taking the steps three at a time. It took a little over two minutes for him to reach the roof access door.

It was locked, but one good kick sent it flying open to rock back and forth on its hinges.

As he charged onto the rooftop, he was caught in a blinding white light and could hear the sound of a police helicopter overhead.

The cavalry had come in full force, only they didn't come to save him. If they caught him, he would go to jail, but worse, his secret identity would be exposed when he was unmasked. His stock would plummet and all the money accumulated made to fight crime would be lost as the stock became worthless.

"Put your hands in the air!" came an electronic voice from overhead, amplified by a bullhorn.

He began to run across the roof, knowing he needed to get out into the open for his escape plan to work. As he ran, he punched in the return code for his jet plane to come back and retrieve him. It was circling continuously in a one mile radius. He could only hope it wasn't a mile out at the moment.

"Cowl, hold it right there or we'll shoot!" came the voice again.

They knew it was him, and with his history with the police, there would be no warning shots.

Darting behind an air conditioning unit, the first bullets peppered the rooftop.

"So much for a warning," the Cowl mumbled under his breath.

Searching the rooftop, he spotted a three inch piece of iron left-over from a welding job on the unit he was hiding behind. After picking it up and hefting it, he ran to the right and popped out into the open. As the spotlight turned to find him, he used the piece of iron like it was one of his Cowlarangs and threw it as hard as he could at the spotlight. His aim was true and it blinked out, glass shards raining down on to the roof as cursing could be heard over the chopper's engine.

More bullets peppered the roof but they were more than six feet from his last location.

Now buying himself some time, he ran out to the far side of the roof, his battle suit and cape allowing him to be just another shadow. He could hear another helicopter approaching, and this one would have a spotlight as well.

He pulled a small balloon from his belt and it inflated when he pressed a button on the small canister attached to it. The lighter than air gas filled the twelve inch balloon and it began to rise. A thin, unbreakable wire filament was attached to it, and as the balloon rose into the night sky, the Cowl attached the other end of the wire to a harness he wore.

Then he had to wait. Sweat trickled under his mask as he counted the seconds. He was entirely exposed but had no choice, he had to remain still.

As the second helicopter approached, the spotlight began to sway back and forth as it searched for him. Once it found him, he would be exposed and a second later would be peppered with armor piercing rounds that even the chest plate on his battle suit couldn't stop.

Then, what he prayed wouldn't happen, did.

The spotlight found him and he raised his right hand to cover his eyes. His jaw was taut as he waited to feel the first impact of a bullet in his chest, but it didn't come.

At the exact instant the trooper in the chopper began to fire, the Cowl's jet plane soared in from the west. On its nose was a pincer, one that caught the balloon and wire, then as the wire slid through the closing pincer, the balloon halted the movement and the wire snapped taut.

On the warehouse roof, the Cowl felt himself yanked into the air. Wind whistled around his ears as just below him, where his feet were only a second ago, the gravel was chopped up by bullets.

He was gone in less than a second, lost in the night sky. The plane banked to the north and his waiting lair.

As he floated in the clear winter sky, the wind cold on his exposed flesh, his entire body aching from his battle with the walking dead, he still felt alive, more alive than he had in years.

The wire began to be retracted and he rose up. He prepared to climb back into the plane, a difficult task when he was at his peak—let alone now—but he knew he would be able to do it.

He wondered idly if the Puppet Master would have truly been able to rule the city with the walking dead.

Pushing the thoughts from his mind, he decided it didn't matter.

The only thing that mattered was he was alive, and once recovered, would soon be back to prowl the night, to take down evil, wherever it might be.

NIGHT OF THE WEREWOLF

A curtain of darkness covered the sprawling metropolis, enveloping it like a shroud. On a lone rooftop in the center of the city overlooking Grand Park, a shadowy figure was perched, his eyes constantly searching for signs of trouble, his ears honing in on anything amiss.

So far it had been a quiet night and the Cowl wasn't complaining. Nights without crime in his beloved city were few and far between, but it was evenings like this when he knew he must be making a difference, that his constant vigil over the city was doing some good.

He shifted slightly, feeling a twinge of pain in his side. The pain was a reminder of his last battle, one where a villain known as the Puppet Master had attempted to rule the city with an army of zombies. But the Cowl had prevailed and the threat had been foiled. But though he had triumphed then, he knew that when one villain was destroyed, a dozen more would pop up.

Supernatural happenings had been occurring far too often for his liking lately. But the Cowl was only a man—albeit a man with an indomitable will and perseverance, and a trust fund that would dwarf the greatest millionaires in the world—with the weaknesses of one, and something had been occurring in his city that made even his iron will tremble.

For how does a man fight magic? How does a man fight the impossible? Deep down he knew the answer: with everything at his disposal, including the kitchen sink. He knew without saying it that no matter what adversary was brought before him, if it threatened his city and the people within it, he would be there to fight back, and to even give his life for the greater good if it came to it.

That was what his parents would have wanted, for him to do what was right, to protect the innocent and punish the guilty; at least that was what he believed, no, he had to believe.

Now long dead from a fatal car crash, his parents' faces still hovered before him in his mind's eye. For a moment he almost reached out with his gloved hand to touch their smiling visages as they floated before him, but then he snapped out of it and shook himself, bringing his attention back to high alert.

Besides, the past was the past, it was gone, lost to the ages, and dwelling on it would gain nothing but sorrow. But then if he didn't dwell on the past, how could he explain what he did every night? How does a man justify running around in a black costume, long dark cape fluttering behind him, a face covered in a mask and more gadgets than even he could use in a single night?

In truth he had no answer, at least not one he wanted to face.

Forcing himself to focus, he reached out with his senses, searching for trouble.

Grand Park was a square mile of lush greenery set into the heart of the city. Though skyscrapers towered on all sides, there was still more than enough space between them to let in the sun during the day.

In the daytime the park was filled with laughing children, joggers, bikers and walkers, as well as the playful sound of barking dogs as they frolicked in the dog park in the very center of the park. Bronze statues of town icons decorated the landscape, and vendors in street-carts sold their wares to passersby.

Filled with people, it was a safe place to be, to enjoy the wonders of life.

But at night the park took on a more sinister veil. Gone were the honest citizens to be replaced by thieves and vagrants. Though the administration had tried to clean up the park at night, it was simply too large and lush to entirety eradicate the seedy element permanently.

When they had finally given up, notices had been placed at all the entrances, informing citizens that to tread through the park at night was a dangerous risk and should be reconsidered before entering.

Of course there were always those who either were too stupid or too oblivious to notice or care, while there were others who thought that nothing bad would ever happen to them.

Such as the young couple who were strolling though the dark pathways of the park, heedless of the danger they could be in. From somewhere off to the right of them a howl permeated the air and the couple stopped walking, their eyes darting back and forth.

"What was that? Maybe we should leave here, Johnny," the girl said as she gripped her boyfriend tighter.

"Aww, lighten up, Lisa," Johnny said. "It was nothin' but a stray dog."

The howl came closer, causing Lisa to all but jump into her lover's arms.

"Lisa, you're shiverin'. Don't worry, baby, I'll protect you. Nothin' can harm you while I'm around." He reached into his pocket, pulled out a small switchblade, and showed it to her. "See? Anyone tries to mess with us and I'll cut 'em good."

Lisa remained silent, her eyes wide, her lips trembling, her bosom heaving. Johnny was what they called a 'bad boy' but though her mother had warned her against boys like him, she still couldn't help herself. She was drawn to Johnny in a way she couldn't explain; it was something about the way he saw life, so carefree and without consequence.

"But if you're still worried, just get a little closer to me," he said as he slid his left hand down to caress her buttocks, his head tilting down so he could press his lips to her full red ones. He could feel her breasts pushing at his chest and it caused him to become aroused, which at his age didn't take much. Just a tad over nineteen, he was young, dumb and full of…well, let's just say 'bravado.'

As their lips met, their surroundings were forgotten, at least for those few seconds, for as soon as they began to kiss, another howl echoed through the park, this one even closer.

Lisa's eyes were closed as she enjoyed the sensation of being so close to Johnny, and of feeling safe in his arms, so because of this, the first sign of trouble she sensed was when Johnny's lips separated from hers and she felt the warm patter of rain on her face as Johnny stepped away from her.

In that brief instant she also detected the smell of wet fur, musky and strong; it reminded her of when her childhood dog 'Dusty' had gone out to pee during a rainstorm and had come inside afterward, its fur wet and dripping.

Then she smelled something else, something coppery with a tinge of iron. Opening her eyes, her mouth fell open and she gasped in horror at the sight before her. On the ground was Johnny, but it was what was on top of him that made her freeze in terror.

She didn't know how to explain what she was seeing, and though deep in her mind she recognized the creature, the part of her mind that believed in sanity and rational thought denied what she saw with her eyes.

But as much as she would have liked to refute what she was seeing, Lisa knew it was real…and it was killing Johnny!

The beleaguered teen had only time for one brief scream of fear before sharp claws ripped his throat out. Gurgling and spitting blood, Johnny looked to Lisa, their eyes locking on one another. Lisa saw desperation in her young lover's eyes, and a pleading for help. Then her glance shifted to the left, where on the ground was Johnny's knife, knocked from his hand when he was tackled.

Fighting her instinct to run, the feeling of protecting Johnny overwhelmed her and Lisa lunged for the knife, grasping it in her ivory-skinned hand and stabbing the beast in the back, just to the right of center and between its shoulder blades.

The beast howled in pain and anger and jumped up, a long hairy arm reaching around to pluck the blade from its back. Looking down at it, the beast studied the weapon for a second, then slowly brought the tip of the knife to its brown lips and licked the tip ever so carefully.

On the ground, Johnny breathed his last.

Blood dripped from the beast's claws as it raised them to its mouth and licked them clean, then, and as if noticing Lisa for the first time, it locked its baleful gaze on her small form.

She stood frozen in horror, petrified to the point that any notion of running was impossible. Her legs weren't her own, her arms like limp noodles, and no matter how much her mind screamed at her to run, to at least try to escape, she couldn't move. Only her heart kept pumping, pushing blood through her body so hard that she felt as if the organ would burst through her chest. In a brief flash she imagined that happening. Her heart would simply push through her ribcage, then out of her skin, the flesh cracking apart like dried leather, then it would spurt from her chest to land at the feet of the mythical creature before her. Then, as she watched, the beast would pick up the heart and devour it, chewing cautiously and enjoying every morsel. And when it was finished with the appetizer, it would tear her apart and feast on the rest of her organs, bloody, sweet and tender from youth.

Reality came crashing back to Lisa as the werewolf howled, tossing the knife to the side as it stood tall on its haunches. It had to be seven feet tall, its entire body covered from head to toe with brown fur. Muscles rippled under that fur, and arms as thick as cordwood flexed as the beast stared at Lisa with hunger in its eyes.

Something in Lisa suddenly freed her and the fugue state of fear that had controlled her so completely was lifted. She began to back away slowly, like she would have done if she'd come upon a stray dog that didn't look safe. The werewolf dropped to all fours and began to follow her, its head low, its haunches flexed to lunge.

In the light of a street lamp, Lisa saw Johnny's cooling corpse one last time and a sob welled up within her. It came out as barely a peep, but to the beast's ears it was like a shout had been elicited. With a growl and a roar, it lunged at Lisa with claws spread wide to rend and tear.

Lisa had time for one last scream before the werewolf was on her.

The Cowl looked to the left as a faint scream carried on the wind. He waited to hear another one so he could pinpoint the exact location but none was forthcoming. But it wasn't truly needed; the scream had come from the park, he was almost positive.

Reaching down to his utility belt, he grabbed his grappling gun, then shot it across the street to a nearby building. The grappling hook wrapped twice around a protruding statue of a menacing gargoyle before the hook caught on the bottom of the stone and clamped on tightly. The Cowl was already in motion by this time, jumping off the building and falling straight to the ground below. When he was ten feet from the pavement, the grappling line went taught and he swung into a dark alley across the street. Pressing a button on the side of the gun, the line was severed. As he ran down the alley, he was already reloading the gun with a new hook and wire for the next time it would be needed. The discarded one would remain where it was until there was a safe time to retrieve it—if at all.

In the side of the alley, almost completely blending into the darkness, was his car: fully armored, self inflating tires and more weapons than most military convoys were armed with.

"Open," he said in a gravelly voice. The car picked up his voice signature immediately and the canopy slid open to reveal the twinkling lights of the nerve center of the rolling arsenal. Climbing onto the frame, he dropped down into the cockpit, for that was the only correct name to describe the seat within the armored car painted entirely in black, including the bulletproof tinted windshield and side windows.

Pressing a button on the dashboard, the car came to life, bright halogen lights pushing back the darkness of the alley. Rats and other vermin near dumpsters and overturned trashcans scattered, wanting to retreat back into the darkness, where it was safe and cool.

Stomping on the gas pedal, the twelve cylinder engine surged and the car jumped forward, the armored vehicle careening out of the alley in a direct line to the closest park entrance.

By the time the last piece of paper and debris had settled back to the alley floor, the rats were back out and on the hunt once more. There was no time to waste when food needed to be found.

The dark sedan pulled up at the north side entrance to Grand Park less than a minute later with a throaty roar from the engine. The Cowl jumped out of the seat and was running as the canopy slid closed behind him.

Most of the street lights were out in the park, something the muggers did to assist in their devious actions, but the Cowl's mask had infra red, which he now used so that the park was as bright as day.

He stopped where four walkways interconnected, unsure of which way to go. Standing tall, he focused his hearing to catch even the slightest sound.

There! The sound of something cracking. A stick perhaps?

Spinning on his black boots, he raced off in the direction of the noise, his right hand reaching down for one of his trusted Cowlarangs, a curved throwing weapon similar to a boomerang, only with razor-sharp tips at both ends. The weapon was more like a throwing star than the former, and was his main choice in his armory to fight evil. Guns were a last resort, for to him, they were a coward's weapon.

As he rounded a bend in the walkway, his right side brushing against untrimmed tree branches that had encroached onto the walk space, he came to a complete halt at the scene before him.

There was the sound of more cracks, and as he stared in horror, what he had believed to be the sound of branches snapping was in reality the noise of bones being shattered to get at the sweet marrow within.

As the Cowl took in the scene before him at a glance, his jaw went taut, for what he saw was once more something that shouldn't exist. It was something of legend, of stories told to children before bed to make them behave, or around campfires to frighten young camp-goers.

No, what crouched on the young woman with her chest torn open and her ribcage separated, what even now was gnawing on one of her ribs like a dog, was none other than a werewolf.

At the same instant the werewolf turned to see the Cowl standing there, the Cowl was already going into action—he threw the Cowlarang at the beast. The weapon soared true and embedded itself into the shoulder of the beast, who howled in pain and prepared to face a new enemy.

But then there were hurried voices floating on the wind and the bouncing of flashlights could be seen further down the path. The unmistakable sound of radio chatter on a police band came as well, though it was muted by distance and volume on the policemen's radios as they ran to investigate the report of screams in the park.

The werewolf roared at the Cowl before spinning around and loping across the ground at intense speed. Not waiting for an invitation, and knowing the police wouldn't understand if they saw him standing over the bodies of the slain couple, the Cowl dashed after the beast, his cape billowing out behind him.

The chase was on.

The werewolf quickly outdistanced its pursuer, but the Cowl was easily able to follow the beast by either its footprints in the dew-covered sod or the way it blundered uncaring through the trees scattered throughout the park. But the beast was fast, and no matter how much The Cowl wanted to reach his prey, the werewolf maintained a good lead.

Where the park ended and opened back onto the city—though on this side it was mostly slums mixed in with abandoned buildings slated for demolition—the trail became all but impossible to see. Taking a second, the Cowl spoke softly into a transmitter at his wrist, giving his car an order to return to his lair. As police surrounded the armored car after finding it, they suddenly jumped back when a small antenna popped up, the engine surged to life and the car drove off, all seemingly on its own. Now on autopilot, the car wouldn't stop until it reached the Cowl's lair.

The Cowl stopped and surveyed the scene before him. Nothing but dilapidated buildings in all directions, many home to crackheads and homeless, as well as other dregs of society that the city had long given up on. As a millionaire many times over, he'd once attempted to help people such as the ones spoken of, but he found out very quickly that no matter how much he spent, no matter how many he tried to help, there were always those that either wanted more for themselves than he could offer, they didn't want his help, or they would have preferred to take the assistance and not done anything in regard to bettering themselves. That was when he learned that one man, no matter how determined and wealthy, still could never save the world; there was simply too much wrong with it.

The crashing of trashcans and the sound of a startled cat floated though the air, of which seemed somehow dirtier in this part of the city, as if the very atmosphere was polluted, the very essence of the place rotten. Racing off in the direction of the disturbance, he crossed the street and dashed into an alley, then charged down it at full speed.

Reaching the end, he stopped and surveyed the area. His eyes caught the glint of spilled liquids, and taking a few steps closer, he found—amidst two overturned trashcans—the carcass of a cat; it had been ripped in half as if it was made of paper.

Even while running from the Cowl, the beast took a moment to feed if opportunity came its way. Searching the ground, the Cowl spotted blood drops, the spacing indicating the way the werewolf had gone. Following slower now, the Cowl carefully made his way down the alley, ears straining to hear anything amiss.

Halfway down the alley he saw that the blood drops turned to the right and stopped. Looking left, all he saw was a cracked brick wall from age, the mortar having fallen to the ground to leave piles of gray dust. On his right was a large faded and chipped green dumpster, the reek of rotten food coming off it enough to make anyone with a sensitive nose want to vomit.

The Cowl stared at the dumpster, his eyes creasing into slits. Pulling out a small penlight, he turned it on, then illuminated the last drop of blood he'd found. Then slowly, the small circular beam of light began to move across the ground, each inch being scrutinized by its owner.

As the light beam reached the edge of the dumpster, it suddenly illuminated a large hairy foot. The beam rose higher, and as it did, the muscular, hairy form the werewolf came into view. Before the Cowl could act, the werewolf was on him, pushing him across the alley until his back came up against the brick wall. Mortar dust rained down on the combatants. Razor-sharp claws began raking the Cowl's body, teeth snapping at his face. His Kevlar-lined battle suit was bulletproof and protected him from the beast's claws, but the teeth snapping at his face was another matter.

He sent blow after blow into the werewolf's body but its powerful form absorbed them easily. Hand to hand, the Cowl was no match for the beast and he knew he needed to back away, to get some breathing room and regroup his attack. But the werewolf was relentless, teeth snapping an inch from his face like a buzz saw, claws constantly raking his armor. The Cowl knew even his armor wouldn't last forever as the razor-sharp claws began to make headway, slowly tearing out grooves of material.

He sent a one-two punch at the beast followed by an uppercut that would have severed the beast's tongue if it had been hanging out of its mouth. The combination of blows would have knocked even the largest fighter down on his butt but barely fazed the werewolf. Still, it gave the Cowl that brief moment he needed to do something drastic.

Reaching down to his utility belt, he pulled out a small three inch canister.

Mace.

As the werewolf lunged at him after recovering from the blows, the Cowl sprayed the mace into the beast's face, blinding it for a moment.

As the werewolf howled in anger and pain, the Cowl extricated himself from between its hairy arms and rolled across the alley to come up in a crouch. His breath came fast as he tried to snap out of the raging fury he had been victim to. The sheer violence of the beast was incredible, the bloodlust overwhelming.

Pulling his grappling hook gun from his belt, he raised it like a handgun and shot the werewolf. The hook missed the beast by inches—which was the plan—then struck the brick wall before rebounding back around, which was when the Cowl yanked on it to get the hook to come back and wrap around the torso of the werewolf. Howling in fury, it attempted to free itself but the line was tested to hold five hundred pounds and was more than a match for the flesh and blood of the beast.

"Down, Fido, heel," The Cowl hissed in his gravelly voice. "Sit!"

The beast fought the wire wrapped around it but it was plain to see even in its rage that the battle was over and the Cowl was victorious. The werewolf howled and raised its snout into the air, as if it was smelling or searching for something.

"Howl all you want, Rover, but this fight is over," the Cowl said as he yanked harder on the wire, trying to topple the beast which defiantly remained upright.

Suddenly, from behind the Cowl, another howl filled the night, then another one. Snapping his head to look behind him, the Cowl's eyes went wide.

"I don't believe it!"

Two more werewolves were loping down the alley at full speed, mouths hanging open, tongues dripping saliva as they raced at the foe that was holding one of their own. Realizing the battle was all but lost—one beast was hard enough to take down let alone three—the Cowl disengaged the grappling hook wire from the gun, reloaded it in the blink of an eye, shot it upward at the edge of the building at his back, and rose into the air.

"Until next time, furballs," he said as he rose out of reach of the beasts. The two werewolves reached the spot the Cowl had occupied a second ago and looked up as their prey disappeared into the night. Then they went to their brother, extricated him of the grappling hook wire, and the three were off, loping down the alley.

The Cowl watched them go for a moment, then followed, this time keeping to the rooftops to remain unnoticed. The buildings were close together, and it was child's play for him to jump from roof to roof as he kept on the trail of the three mythical creatures.

Eventually, the three werewolves stopped in another filthy alleyway. The Cowl crouched down, his form all but hidden in the night, his cape wrapped tightly around him to add to the camouflage. One of the new arrivals bent down and removed a manhole cover with ease, the other two climbing down into the darkness of the hole, then it too followed, dragging the cover behind it. The solid steel cover seated into the hole with a dull thud and all was silent with the exception of the usual city sounds of the city's slums, such as the faint cry of a hungry baby, a car horn and a screech of tires.

The Cowl went to a fire escape on the side of the building and climbed down, then walked over to the manhole cover. His eyes took in the number etched on the cover—which denoted its location—the street names of the adjoining roads that connected with the alley, and any building that consisted of a name or title, then he turned and was off, soon lost in the night yet again.

Now that he knew where they'd gone, he would be back, but first he needed to return to his lair and prepare himself for the coming battle.

Three hours later, a sleek motorcycle roared down the lonely road leading away from the Cowl's lair. Painted in midnight black, the sides were covered with protuberances. In these were everything from a small rocket compartment to a flame thrower to smoke grenades. The front of the motorcycle had five halogen lights mounted to the frame and handlebars. The back of the bike was stacked with luggage compartments filled with tools and other assorted items that the Cowl deemed might be needed this night.

After calling for a pickup and returning to his lair, the Cowl had gone through sewer maps of the city, finding the best entrance that would lead him to the general vicinity of the manhole cover. From there he would rely on his tracking skills to find the were-wolves.

On the west side of the city was an abandoned aqueduct, and it was here that he drove. Upon arriving, it was a simple task to cut the lock on the large metal grate and drive inside, the halogen lights keeping the darkness at bay.

The under-city was a world unto itself, filled with abandoned subway tunnels that went on for miles in every direction and large caverns left over from the development of the city decades ago. Long ago, foundations had been made and the ground excavated, only to have developers find out that the area was unstable and littered with sinkholes. These areas had been concreted over and made into parking lots after reinforcing the ground with massive steel beams to support the weight of the vehicles above, which left caverns the size of football fields below.

In the winter months decades ago, the homeless, seeking warmth, turned to going underground to survive, and over time, large groups had sprung up, including criminals escaping justice and other outcasts of society that had joined them later. But after so many years of living in almost perpetual darkness, they had devolved into creatures just a step above animals, who were light sensitive and hated what they called the 'norms' that lived above them, and who were ignorant of the plight of the dwellers below.

The Cowl slowed his motorcycle as he surveyed the area at the end of the tunnel leading from the aqueduct. Before him stood the ruins of a building and piles of trash. Vermin scurried about, searching for food, and for a brief moment when he turned his head, he thought he spotted the tail of an alligator slithering into a pile of refuse, but he may have been wrong. Even a man with a will as strong as the Cowl's could be spooked in a place like the under-city.

Checking his map, he picked the best possible tunnel that would lead him where he wanted to go, then after stowing the map in his utility belt, he began riding.

The Cowl shifted on his seat to get more comfortable as he drove through the Stygian darkness of yet another subway tunnel, only the halogen lights keeping the darkness from surrounding him in its cold blanket. The new suit he wore chafed here and there, the leather needing to be broken in. His old suit was ruined, the claws of the werewolf having done massive damage to the material, and even though it had been Kevlar, if he hadn't stopped the beast when he did, the claws would have penetrated his suit eventually and shredded his flesh into bloody ribbons.

It had been more than three hours since he'd entered the under-city and he'd found and then lost the trail of the werewolves multiple times. Checking his watch, he saw it was going on morning on the surface but here underground, time was meaningless. It was always night when there was no sun.

He had come across some of the dwellers of this world of perpetual night a few times, but it had been easy to chase them away with the use of flares or simply blinding them with his halogens beams. They were mostly scavengers and had no stomach for a fight, especially not with an enemy that was as prepared for battle as the Cowl. So they ran off, scurrying away like rats to find easier prey.

Suddenly, over the soft purring of the motorcycle's modified and almost silent engine, he heard another sound. As he stopped the bike and listened, the rumbling began to grow louder until it was almost right on top of him. Looking down, he realized he was riding on one of the old subway tracks, and on further inspection after shining light on the parallel steel rails, he saw that the tracks were in good condition, and had been patched up where needed to become serviceable.

It was as he came to this conclusion that a light began to shine from a bend in the tunnel and the rumbling grew even louder.

It wasn't hard to figure out what was happening, and spinning around, the Cowl began driving back the way he'd come, while behind him, the subway car bore down on him, gaining with every second.

The rats scattered as the black motorcycle shot out of the tunnel, only a fraction of a second before the subway car plowed over him. The Cowl jumped the tracks, fighting the front wheel as if it was a living thing and barely managed to remain upright. Skidding to a halt in a spray of refuse and gravel, he found himself in a different cavern than before. He must have taken another tunnel in his haste to escape the barreling subway car.

Taking it all in at a glance, he first saw that the cavern was huge, the light from his headlights barely touching the ceiling. All around him were pieces of subway cars, a junkyard filled with the cast-offs of locomotion.

But he only had a split second to take all this in before the subway car that was chasing him came roaring out of the tunnel. The machine had been modified. The engine was still in front, but the back end, where the driver had once been housed, had been sheared off at waist height so it was open to the air. All around the control area where the operator stood, were a dozen men and even a few women. All were hard-looking, with eyes that were cold and menacing. These weren't the regular scum, the scavengers that the Cowl had run into before, these were some of the escaped criminals and outcasts. All were hard men and women who had no problem with a fight, and in fact relished one more so than simply taking what they wanted without effort.

Though the cavern was a sight in itself, all this was nothing compared to what the Cowl saw strapped to the front of the engine, smack dab between the two circular headlights.

"I don't believe it, a white werewolf!" he exclaimed.

"Look at that idiot in a costume!" one of the criminals cried out.

"Who cares," another said. "Look at that bike he's on. We get that and we'll have the run of this place."

"You'll get this bike over my dead body," the Cowl said as the subway car came to a screeching stop.

"That was the plan, 'norm,' we wouldn't want it any other way," another said as the group of convicts pulled an assortment of weapons out and aimed them at the Cowl.

On the front of the train, the white werewolf roared in anger, wanting to break free of its bonds. Its muscles rippled under its fur, straining to escape, but the straps holding it were too strong.

The Cowl, seeing this, pulled a Cowlarang from his utility belt and threw it with precision at the werewolf, the tip of the 'rang slicing into the strap holding the beast's left arm. The strap let go with a loud *snap* and with one arm free and claws extended, the werewolf made short work of the remaining straps holding it. In an instant it was lunging off the car and running away, its powerful leg muscles covering ground easily.

"The werewolf's free!" one of the convicts cried out. "Kill it before it escapes!"

"Not on my watch," the Cowl said. "I need that beastie alive." The thumb of his right hand shifted slightly to a row of toggle switches mounted on the handle bar. A moment later, two tear gas canisters were fired from hidden tubes on each side of the motorcycle. The canisters arced through the air to land directly in the center of the convicts. Chaos ensued as they began coughing and gagging, their eyes watering to the point they couldn't see. A few fired their weapons wildly, shooting each other by accident.

The Cowl barely saw any of this; he'd already spun the motorcycle around and was chasing the white werewolf down an intersecting tunnel. As he rode, he reached down with his left hand to touch the gun strapped to his thigh. The revolver was loaded with bullets that were tipped with silver. In one of his side bags on the bike he also carried another two dozen more rounds of ammunition, the tips of the bullets also dipped in silver. He had seen three werewolves before coming down into the under-city, and there was no way to know if there were more, so he made sure to come ready for anything. The gun was a last resort, but he knew he would use it if there was no other choice.

But this white werewolf he now chased was something else all together. He didn't know where the beast would lead him, whether it was part of the others he'd fought or was alone, but he knew he wouldn't get any answers if he didn't capture it first. So wrapping his hands around the handlebars and kicking the bike into the next gear, he raced after the white werewolf, knowing he would follow it wherever it led.

The Cowl slowed the motorcycle as he approached an open area where torches flickered, the howling of a wolf informing him to use caution. Then, he turned off the engine and rolled up silently with the headlights off until he had a clear view of the landscape before him.

Another large cavern was ahead, and in the middle of it was a giant boulder. On this makeshift dais stood the white werewolf, and surrounding the beast on all sides had to be two dozen more werewolves, all of the brown persuasion.

The white werewolf titled back its head and howled, the others mimicking it. Clawed hands were raised into the air, the brown werewolves cheering for their leader.

"Looks like there's a rally going on," the Cowl said under his breath. His mind raced with how he was going to deal with so many foes at once, especially when each individual was more than a match for him.

But then the decision on how to proceed was taken from him as another werewolf arriving late to the party spotted the dark figure on the motorcycle on the edge of the clearing. The werewolf let out a high-pitched howl that had all the others turning as one, yellow eyes locking onto the newfound prey.

"That's not good," the Cowl said, and as the werewolves charged at him, he turned his headlights on full blast and started the engine. As the first werewolf in line reached him, the glare of the headlights blinded it, and the boot to its chest sent it flying backwards. The Cowl drove straight into the pack, knowing a full on attack was his only chance at survival. The beasts didn't expect that, they expected him to turn and run.

Twin bike cannons popped put of the front of the motorcycle and began firing, the bullets tearing into bodies and shredding flesh as fur went flying in all directions. But the ammunition was standard, no silver on its tips, and all it did was slow down the pack, not kill them for good. But even a mythical creature isn't going to do too well when hit with a dozen rounds of high-powered bullets.

"Down, Fido!" he yelled as he elbowed a werewolf in the face, feeling canines crack and shatter from the blow. "Bad dog!" he shouted at another as he clubbed it on the back of the head with his fist. But fighting and driving was almost impossible, as his right hand had to stay on the throttle at all times, for if his speed dropped he would be swarmed instantly and then it would be all over.

With a press of a toggle switch he sent out more tear gas and added smoke grenades, the entire area filling in seconds with a toxic cloud. Pulling a respirator from inside his armored suit, he sucked in the clean oxygen and continued the fight. Through the haze of smoke he searched for the white werewolf, and upon finding it, began riding in the beast's direction, while continually punching and kicking at brown figures that became indistinguishable in the smoke.

But it worked and the werewolves backed off, most choking and gagging on the tear gas. It wasn't a permanent solution but it was good in the interim.

The white werewolf, seeing things weren't going as planned, turned and sprinted away, but the Cowl was hot on its trail again. A brown werewolf leaped out of the smoke coming right at the Cowl but he riddled it full of holes while yelling, "Play dead, Rover, I'm coming through!"

The Cowl pulled a pin on a grenade and tossed it over his shoulder into the thickest of the werewolf pack. "Fetch!" he yelled as the grenade went off, sending pieces of werewolf in all directions. The rest of the pack halted its chase and surveyed the scene. Deciding that the peril of chasing the Cowl wasn't worth the risk, they turned and began feeding on their fallen brethren, fighting amongst themselves for whatever piece of warm meat could be found.

"That'll hold 'em for a while," he said to himself as he glanced over his shoulder. Then he turned forward and focused once more on the chase at hand.

There was a winding path between the rubble and debris lining the ground and the Cowl drove through it as fast as possible, trying to make up the lead the white werewolf had on him. But haste was never a good thing when following something primal, and cornering it could be even worse. Five minutes after leaving the werewolf pack behind, he was caught off guard when the werewolf turned the tables on him and attacked from out of the shadows. One second the Cowl was astride his motorcycle, the next he was flying through the air in the clutches of the beast, the bike falling onto its side without a rider.

Before he could do anything to protect himself, he felt a sharp pain in his right shoulder as the werewolf sank its razor-sharp teeth into his flesh. Crying out in agony, he let out the remaining air in his lungs as he hit the ground hard, the white werewolf on top of him. Biting back the pain, he slid his legs up to his chest so that they were between him and the beast, then kicked out with all the strength he had left. The werewolf was thrown from the Cowl to land on its back ten feet away. It rolled to its feet instantly, and while licking its lips of the blood coating its mouth, it growled and prepared to lunge at its prey. The Cowl's right arm was useless, the wound having done damage to muscles and tendons, and he fought to stand upright as shock washed over him. The bite was deep and he could feel the blood seeping under his suit, already becoming sticky as it coated his skin.

Shaking the stars from his eyes, he focused on his enemy. Not thinking about the gun on his hip and only acting on instinct, he pulled a Cowlarang with his left hand and threw it at the werewolf. It flew true and struck the beast in the center of its chest. The werewolf barked in anger and brushed the 'rang from its chest, a small blood stain marring its fur from where the sharp tip had penetrated. The Cowl regretted not coating his 'rangs with silver as well, but there had only been so much time and the bullets should have been more than enough.

The bullets! The gun!

He wasn't thinking straight, he should have gone for that first but now he knew that was his only hope.

The wolf charged at him and the Cowl reached around his waist with his good hand and pulled the gun off his right hip. The movement was awkward and the extra moment it took to draw the gun was more than enough time for the werewolf to attack yet again. The Cowl was knocked off his feet to land in the dirt, the gun flying off to land somewhere in the darkness. His wound flared up each time he moved his right arm, causing bright light to dance before his vision. Off to the right of where he lay, his motorcycle was on its side, the rear tire still spinning as the engine kept running. The headlights were still on and provided illumination, otherwise the entire area would have been nothing but darkness.

The beast attacked again, clawing at the Cowl's chest, only the Kevlar saving him from evisceration. With his good hand he punched the werewolf in the side but what would have incapacitated a man did nothing against the beast. Becoming desperate, his hand flailed out for something to use as a weapon and only found a rock slightly bigger than his fist. But he wasn't in a position to turn anything down, so he grabbed the rock and brought it up and around in a wide arc. The rock connected solidly with the werewolf's temple, and in a whine resembling a hurt dog, the beast was knocked off the Cowl to fall onto its side. It got to its knees quickly however and crawled away, not wanting to be struck again.

The Cowl got to his knees, his vision worse than before. He shook his head, not understanding what was wrong with him. Though the wound was deep, it shouldn't have been incapacitating him like it was.

Then he saw the white werewolf watching him, not attacking but only staring at him, and as he also came to his knees, he felt a massive pain in his stomach, one that filled him from his head to his toes.

Everything hurt; his skin, his limbs, even his hair screamed out in agony. What was wrong with him? Why did he feel this way?

And then realization dawned on him and it chilled him to his very soul. He'd been bitten, he was cursed, and if he didn't do something quickly, he was going to turn into a werewolf like the pack he'd left behind. He could already feel the change beginning. Soon he would be nothing but a mindless beast, his very essence lost to a primal spirit that would take full control over him.

His hazed mind began to work overtime on some way to prevent this from happening. He thought back to the research he'd done before setting off to the under-city, about all he'd read about werewolves and the curse.

One way to break the curse was to kill the werewolf that bit you. He didn't know if this was true but he didn't really have a choice. But he'd lost the gun with the silver-tipped bullets, and though he had more ammunition on the motorcycle, a fat lot of good it would do without the gun.

The gun—he had to retrieve it.

Guessing in the direction the weapon had fallen, he ran there as fast as he could, his breath coming in quick gasps. The werewolf attempted to stop him but the Cowl was faster. The desperation-fueled adrenalin pumping through his system made him even faster than the powerful creature.

By pure dumb luck he'd picked the right way, and in the headlamps of the motorcycle, the metal gleam of the gun winked from between two rocks. The Cowl lunged for the gun, and as he brought it up to fire—the white werewolf only a few feet away and closing rapidly—the Cowl squeezed the trigger.

But there was no gunshot, not even a dry click to mark the action. Something inside the weapon had failed and the gun had misfired—there would be no second chance to rectify the mistake.

Then the werewolf struck him, sending the Cowl flying away to land heavily on his back. The gun fell from his hand, bounced across the ground, and dropped into a hole so deep that the sound of it landing didn't come to the Cowl's ears, though he tried to focus on hearing it land.

Once more he was battling with the hairy beast and once more only his iron will allowed him to escape alive. As the werewolf tried to bite his face off, the Cowl raised his left arm up and jammed it into the werewolf's mouth, breaking teeth and jamming it there. Then, with all his strength, he leveraged himself up and to the side. When he yanked his arm free, the werewolf came down and hit the ground hard, missing the Cowl by less than an inch. The Cowl rolled away and knew that his time was almost over. He was out of will, out of energy and out of luck.

He laid prone on the ground, breathing hard, blood filling the inside of his suit, his right arm almost useless, as he watched the white werewolf roll onto its back and then get to its feet.

The Cowl felt something pressing into his back, and though he had no more fight left, he slowly reached around and under him with his left hand, figuring his last moments shouldn't be spent with something jabbing him in the back. His hand wrapped around something long and thin, and though he didn't know what it was, he knew it was in the shape of something that could be used as a weapon.

But he had to bide his time. He would only get one chance, and if he didn't time it perfectly he would lose it.

"Come on, Whitey, let's end this here and now," he hissed through gritted teeth, his hand gripping the hidden weapon even tighter.

The werewolf growled in such a way that the Cowl swore it sounded like laughter, then the beast came charging at him. The Cowl remained perfectly still, as if he was prey that had accepted defeat. Then, at the last possible second, when it was too late for the werewolf to stop its forward momentum, the Cowl pulled out the weapon he had hidden under him.

It was a piece of rebar about three feet long, and as the beast lunged forward, its feet leaving the ground, its claws reaching outward to rent and kill, the Cowl rolled to the side and jammed the end of the rebar into the ground and aimed the other end at the approaching beast. The werewolf's eyes went wide as it realized what was about to happen.

The weight of the beast was more than enough to do the job, and as it came down on the rebar, the tip pierced its chest dead center, the body then sliding down onto the shaft. But the Cowl knew this wouldn't stop the beast for good so he reached out, grabbed a decent-sized rock with his good hand, and raised it high in the air and brought it down hard on the werewolf's head. For the second time in as many minutes the werewolf was bludgeoned with a rock and this time the blow knocked it unconscious.

Sucking in air, and fighting consciousness himself, the Cowl got to his knees and then stood up. Though swaying back and forth like he was drunk, he remained standing. He ignored the pain filling his body and went to his fallen motorcycle. Reaching into one of the compartments, he pulled out a medical kit and shot himself full of adrenaline, antibiotics and vitamin B-12, anything that would keep him conscious for just a little while longer.

As the chemicals flooded his system, his head cleared slightly and though he could still feel the curse suffusing his veins, he picked up his bike, turned off the engine, and put it on its kickstand. His legs got weak and he used the bike to stabilize himself, and when the weakness passed and he knew he wasn't going to fall over, he moved away from it. His gaze fell on the prone werewolf, lying motionless but still breathing. He had to figure out a way to kill it and fast, before he changed himself, and he also needed to destroy the entire wolf pack. But how?

Then his eyes widened as an idea came to him.

It was a slim hope but slim was better than nothing.

With every muscle and tendon in his body aching in pain, he got to work, knowing time was far shorter than he wanted it to be.

With haste born from the dread of knowing his coming fate, the doomed man drove his motorcycle back the way he'd come, searching for one particular spot in the ceiling. On the back of the bike, lying with its stomach on the seat and its head and legs hanging off the sides, was the white werewolf.

I know the spot is around here somewhere, the Cowl thought as his high beams pushed away the darkness. The chemical cocktail he'd pumped his body full of was already wearing off and he knew he had less than ten minutes before he went into total meltdown. Already his head was becoming cloudy, his vision growing fuzzy, his muscles twitching as they prepared to transform him into a hairy brute that wanted to do nothing but hunt and kill.

And then he found the spot he wanted. Overhead, the ceiling of the cavern was nothing but jagged rock and protruding pipes from old foundations of the surface city. Holes could be seen here and there, and from the way it looked, one good blast would have it all come tumbling down in an avalanche of rock, dirt and cement.

The Cowl stopped the motorcycle directly under the worst part of the ceiling and got off it, using the kickstand to keep it upright, then he propped the white werewolf on the seat as if it was riding the bike. He then leaned over the beast and pressed another switch. This one controlled a built-in recorder. Earlier, when the white werewolf had howled loudly to the wolf pack as it stood upon the dais, the Cowl's bike had recorded it, as it did all missions. Normally this was so he could go through the mission and study it more closely, and by doing so see where he made mistakes so he could correct them. But now, the record of his foray into the under-city was going to be used for a far more important purpose.

Upon pressing the switch, the blood-curdling howl of the white werewolf sounded from hidden speakers on the motorcycle. The Cowl hobbled away to a safe distance—or what he hoped was a safe distance—and waited for the wolf pack to arrive, all the while holding back the change by sheer force of his iron will.

The wail of the white werewolf floated through the tunnels and caverns of the under-city. Upon hearing this, wherever they were located, the wolf pack stopped what they were doing and returned the call, then loped off in the direction of their leader.

Hidden between a pile of rubble, the Cowl heard the cries of the answering wolf pack echo through the tunnels and nodded.

Good, they're coming, but will they get here in time before I change? he wondered as he fought to stay conscious. In his hand he held a small detonator, a red button in the center of the black box. All he had to do was press it and the self-destruct on the motorcycle would be activated and it would explode. All his machines had self-destruct options built into them: the car, the helicopter, his jet and the motorcycle. He could never allow his weapons to get into the wrong hands—never.

Hurry up, you mangy bags of fur, before I'm too far gone to press the button, he thought.

Then the first werewolf arrived, loping across the ground; it was followed by even more. From across the area others came out of adjoining tunnels as well, all of them racing to join their leader, the white werewolf.

Seconds later, the entire pack was gathered around their leader, who was even now coming to. The white werewolf looked down at itself, not understanding where it was or how it got to be surrounded by its brethren. The beast opened its mouth to howl a warning to the others, to tell them that something wasn't right, that they need to leave before it was too…

From across the cavern, hidden in a pile of rubble, a clawed hand covered in fur pressed the detonator button, one last act of defiance before the mind of its owner was lost in the curse of blood and fury.

The motorcycle self-destructed, sending shrapnel off in all directions, but most of all, the bullets with silver tips in the side compartments were shot outward to pierce every single werewolf within the blast radius.

The shockwave also went straight up, hitting the ceiling and shattering the tenuous hold there. A heart beat after the motorcycle exploded, thousands of tons of rock and gravel began to pour down and bury the carcasses of the werewolves in a grave that would never be disturbed.

Off to the side, the Cowl—or what was once known as the Cowl—let out a howl of triumph as the tons of debris rained down on his foes, killing them all, and even if not, then trapping them forever in a tomb of rock and dirt.

As the massive dust cloud filled the cavern, the werewolf once known as the Cowl stumbled out of hiding and surveyed the scene of devastation, his nose twitching as he tried to detect prey, but no sooner did he do this than he fell to knees and curled up in pain.

Howling in agony once more, he began to transform back to his human form. Hair retracted, his snout withdrew, and sharp claws slid back into his fingers, until the beast was gone and only an exhausted, pain-filled man remained.

He tried to stand but got no farther than raising his head, then his face slumped back into the dirt and he was lost in oblivion.

Time held no meaning for the Cowl, but eventually he came to, and spitting dirt from cracked and dry lips, he sat up, holding his head in his good hand, his right arm so stiff it was pretty much useless.

He was surrounded by darkness. He reached into his utility belt with his good hand and pulled out a pen light. Turning it on, he saw the fresh rubble of the ceiling collapse and it all came flooding back to him He looked down at his hands, relieved to see they were human between where the gloves he wore had split open as his hands had grown with the transformation.

But the white werewolf had been destroyed in the blast, and because it had been at the epicenter, no doubt it had been vaporized, and though the curse had changed the Cowl, the destruction of the beast had allowed him to revert back to normal.

He sat there for a while, just glad to be alive, and when he thought he was strong enough, he got to his feet, pulled out the map of the under-city, found the closest exit to where be thought he was, and headed off.

He needed medical attention desperately. He had people for that; doctors who would help him for a fee and never ask any questions. He would be fine…in time. For time healed all wounds, whether mental or physical.

Slowly, he limped his way back to the surface.

PLAYTIME WITH THE TOYMAKER

Night hung over the city in a dark blanket filled with deadly shadows between buildings. The sprawling metropolis was changing over from the routine of the day, with mothers bringing children to school, and workers going to and from work, to the evening party crowd filled with revelers and drinkers, eager to taste the night life that the city had to offer.

But another type of character came out as the sun dropped from the sky. The predator, who hoped to prey on those only wanting to have fun and enjoy life. Muggers, thieves and rapists prowled the streets of the city this night, but they weren't the only ones.

One more soul watched the city streets, this one with a heart as cold and dark as the predators. But there was one very important difference between him and them.

His soul was on the side of justice.

The Cowl scanned the street below, his eyes taking in the marquees of the theater district. Two squad cars were below him, their blue dome lights flashing, pushing back the few shadows that managed to survive under the neon signs on every corner. There had been a mugging but the police were nearby and had caught the criminal, and were even now placing him in the back seat of one of the squad cars. A minute later, the car with the mugger drove off, a few bleeps of the siren sounding to make gawkers and lookeeloos get out of the way.

When he was satisfied there was no need for him, the Cowl pulled his grappling hook gun from his belt, shot the cable to the next building, and stepped off the rooftop he'd been on. The cool night air rushed past his face, getting beneath his mask and cooling the sweat trapped within.

His legs swung out before him, close together, and like a spear he sliced through the night and landed on the next rooftop. He disengaged the cable and connected a new coil onto the end of the grappling gun, then hooked it back onto his utility belt. The belt was filled with small compartments where all manner of gadgetry was at his disposal.

But the most important weapon in the Cowl's arsenal was his own skill as a fighter. Trained in martial arts, his body honed to peak perfection, he was an incredible fighting machine for the force of good.

Inner demons made him do what he did, and some would call him insane if they knew who he was and why he did the things he chose to do on a nightly basis. But when the sun began to rise on a new day, and he went back to his lair to sleep, he slept the slumber of the righteous, of a man who knew he had made a difference that night.

After studying the street below, the Cowl began to run across the roof. If someone was to look up, they would have seen a dark figure silhouetted against the moonlit sky, but before they had a chance to call out, perhaps tell another of what they'd spied, the figure was gone, lost amongst the rooftops.

The Cowl was attired entirely in black, the tough leather made into a Kevlar-lined suit that covered him from head to toe, only his lower jaw exposed to the air. Billowing out behind him was a cape of midnight blue, which in the darkness blended perfectly, and in fact even better than if it was black. The leather was malleable and flexed with him, and other than the Kevlar sewn into the material, he was entirely vulnerable against an attacker's weapons. But that was assuming an attacker had a chance to fire a gun or lunge at him with a blade. His reflexes were sharp to the point of being supernatural, and it was the rare mugger or murderer who ever so much as laid a finger on him.

Suddenly, the Cowl heard someone scream in either fear or pain from the next street over. Reaching his hand up to his ear, he touched the small amplifier sewn into the mask. Like a hearing aid only a thousand times more powerful, the Cowl could separate out the ambient noise of the city and hone in on one specific sound. He did so now, tracking the origination of the scream. The amplifier was so powerful he could hear a pin drop on the street below if he boosted the power high enough. But he had to be careful; if he was focusing on something soft at the same time a truck blew its horn in the same vicinity, he could blow out his eardrum.

The scream came again and he was able to pinpoint its location exactly. Stepping off the rooftop, he plummeted to the street below. His cape flapped out around him, the Mylar material catching the air like a parachute and hang glider combined.

He soared over the street, and if anyone would have glanced up, all they would have seen was a dark blur contrasting against the neon lights of the city. Then he was in the alley across the street and touching down softly, already running at full speed.

Rounding a bend in the alley, he came upon four men all in black wearing ski masks and gloves, each one holding some sort of weapon.

On the ground on her stomach was a woman with long blonde hair. Her face was covered by her hair so that the Cowl didn't know how badly she was hurt. He could see she wasn't moving, however, which meant she'd already been attacked.

Though the faces of the four men were covered, the Cowl was able to classify them by size and height. The first one was a stocky fellow a little over five feet, with a stump for a neck. The second man was skinny, like a stick, with skin as white as a sheet where it showed—places such as the wrists, where there was a break between his glove and jacket, and his neck and around the eyes and lips where the mask didn't cover.

The third man was fat, though pudgy would have been a better description. He had two chins that could easily be seen even beneath his mask. The Cowl could see the sweat around his eyes, the exertion of the attack causing the fat man to perspire.

The last man stood with confidence and carried himself with confidence. Beneath his black attire muscles rippled. He stood a little over six feet tall with broad shoulders and fists the size of pot roasts. His skin was dark under the mask, so he was either black or perhaps of Latin decent. The Cowl knew instantly that the last man would be the most formidable.

None of the men carried guns, only knives and bludgeoning instruments.

"Leave now and you won't get hurt," the Cowl said, his voice cold and raspy.

"Hey, look at the nutjob in the Halloween costume," the pudgy man laughed.

"Last warning," the Cowl said, taking a step forward.

"The only one gettin' hurt 'round here is gonna be you," the stocky man with a stump for a neck said.

"Fine with me." The Cowl went into action, sprinting towards the four men, getting in their midst before they knew the Cowl had even moved. The first one to go down was the skinny man, sent to the ground with a karate kick to the right knee. The sound of the kneecap snapping filled the alley and the man fell hard. He let out a wail and pulled his knee to his chest, holding it with his arms. He rocked back and forth, wailing that he was hurt. The knife he'd been holding fell to the ground as well.

Sweeping his leg under the next man—the fat and pudgy one—the Cowl brought the man to his butt easily. He would have finished the man off with a blow to the head, but the tall man with the muscular build came at him, wrapping long arms around the Cowl's chest and squeezing. The Cowl could feel his ribcage compressing. His opponent was indeed a powerful fighter.

The stocky man stepped in and started using the crowbar he carried to whack the Cowl in the abdomen, just below the tall man's arms. The blows knocked the wind from the Cowl, but the leather and Kevlar suit prevented any real damage. Still, if it didn't stop soon, the blows would eventually cause harm.

The Cowl raised his left boot and brought it down hard on the tall man's instep. The man howled in pain and let go of the Cowl, then hopped away.

Now free, the Cowl began to punch and kick at the stocky man, blow after blow sending the man falling backwards to land in a pile of cardboard boxes. Picking up a full garbage can, the Cowl brought it down on top of the stocky man's head, knocking the would-be mugger out cold.

A yell and heavy footsteps caused the Cowl to spin around to see the pudgy man coming at him with a baseball bat. Reaching down to his utility belt, the Cowl pulled a Cowlarang and threw it at the man's legs. The 'rang he used had a thin line attached to it, the weight on the line good for up to a thousand pounds. The 'rang zipped by the man, trailing the line, then like a boomerang, it looped back, the line catching on the man's legs to then wrap around and around three times.

The man's legs became tangled and he began to fall forward. Not smart enough to release the bat so he could stop his fall, he plummeted to the ground and the bat hit the pavement first, before it bounced off the pavement to smack him in the forehead, then snapped back to the ground again, where he struck the bat one more time and went prone. His forehead bleeding through the ski mask, he lay in and out of consciousness, as the sound of wood bouncing off asphalt and skull faded away.

A roar from behind was the only warning the Cowl had that the muscular man had recovered from his wounded leg and was attacking. A blow from a fist the size of a small ham landed on the Cowl's back and once more only his battle suit protected him from a broken back. But still, the Cowl went to his knees from the force of the punch.

"Now you die, nutjob," the muscular man hissed as he raised his hands over his head, clasping them together to make one giant fist. When that two-hand blow came down on the Cowl's head, even his suit and years of training wouldn't prevent him from suffering a broken neck.

But the Cowl hadn't survived as long as he had by not being able to get out of a bad situation. As the hands came down, the Cowl did what the muscular man never would have expected. He stood up, his head going right into the clasped hands as they dropped. But the force of the impact was a fraction of what it would have been, given that the man hadn't had time to bring the full force of his powerful physique behind the blow.

So instead of suffering a broken neck, the Cowl was merely dazed, a ringing filling his ears as he rolled away and to the side. He didn't care where he went, he just needed a few seconds to gather his wits. To ensure this, he reached down and pulled a smoke pellet from his utility belt, then slammed it down onto the ground. Instantly, the alley began to fill with smoke, but there was a strong wind and already it began to disperse.

Seconds went by as the muscular man waved his hand in front of his face to get the smoke out of his eyes. He peered into the thinning cloud, searching for his foe so he could finish the job.

Squinting slightly to see, he bent over just a little, as if that would help his vision. Off and to the side, the man with the broken kneecap still wailed for someone to help him. Then the man's eyes went wide as a black-gloved fist shot out of the smoke cloud and into his jaw. The man stumbled backwards and went down hard, unconscious before he hit the pavement.

The Cowl stepped out of the thinning cloud and gazed down at the tall man. It appeared that his foe, though muscular, had a glass jaw.

Deciding he didn't want any more surprises, the Cowl pulled a plastic zip tie from his utility belt and secured the man's hands behind his back. Then, deciding to err on the side of caution, he took two more zip ties and wrapped the man's wrists again, then did the same to his legs. Now fully hog-tied, the man was definitely no longer a threat.

Standing up, the Cowl looked around the alley, knowing the fight was over. Three men were out cold and the other was wailing on the ground, hugging his knee and crying like a baby.

The woman was still laying face-down on the ground, too, and he went to her now, kneeling by her side. Careful when moving her in case she was seriously hurt, he slowly rolled her over so that her head was on his lap. There was no blood, which was good, and there didn't appear to be any wounds to her head. He assumed she must have fainted.

"Easy there, miss, you're safe now. Are you hurt?" he asked softly.

Her eyes were closed, her lips slightly open. He could see she was pretty, and he wondered how she'd managed to wind up in an alley being accosted by four masked men. Perhaps she'd taken the alley as a shortcut to find out it had been a serious mistake.

When she didn't respond, he brushed the hair from her eyes and asked, "Miss, are you all right?"

He was taken completely off guard when her eyes suddenly snapped open and she replied, "I'm fine, honey, but you're not." Her hand came up and around so that it was in front of the Cowl. She was holding a small canister with a trigger that she pressed, the canister spraying knockout gas right into his face.

Coughing as he inhaled the gas, he dropped her and crawled away, trying to get to clean air. Reaching up to his face, he pressed a hidden button in his mask that released pure oxygen from tiny tubes sewn into the battle suit that were connected to oxygen canisters in his utility belt. The idea was to have the air blowing out of his mask and into his nose and mouth so that noxious fumes around him couldn't get in, but he'd breathed in too much of the knockout gas already.

Though he tried to fight it, his vision began to blur and he collapsed to the ground, only managing to turn over with the last of his remaining strength.

He saw the woman he'd thought he was saving standing over him, a cruel smile on her lips. As the Cowl finally succumbed to the gas and fell into oblivion, he could hear her laughing.

The Cowl awoke slowly, his mind groggy from the gas. At first he didn't know where he was. Then it all came flooding back and he forced his eyes to focus.

He was inside the back of a cargo van, his arms tied up behind him with rope. His utility belt was hanging on the back of the passenger seat.

Craning his neck, he looked up to see who was driving. He could only see the side of the man's face but from the dark skin and muscular arms, he had a pretty good idea who it was. Shifting his gaze to the passenger seat, he saw it was the woman who had gassed him.

They were arguing about something. But with the noise of the engine, coupled with the bouncing of the shocks on the vehicle, it was hard to focus on what they were saying. Still, he was able to use the hearing amplifier in his ear to pull their voices out of the other sounds. He pressed his head to the ridged floor, and after a few seconds, managed to engage the button to turn on the amplifier.

"I just don't see why we can't have a look under his mask," the muscular man said.

"It doesn't matter what you think," the woman replied. "The Toymaker said we don't touch him once we captured him. Now, I don't know about you, but I know better than to cross him."

"Ah, the Toymaker ain't so tough," the man said.

The woman shifted in her seat so she was looking directly at the driver. The Cowl could see her profile as she said, "You better watch what you say, Ralph. The Toymaker has ears everywhere. He could even be hearing everything you're saying right now."

Ralph swallowed hard. "You think?" He paused. "Uh, listen, I guess I was wrong. The Toymaker's always right," he backpedaled.

The woman smiled. "Right; now just get us back to the hideout and no more talking."

A few minutes went by and then Ralph said, "I still don't get why we had to capture this guy." He gestured with his chin to the rear of the cargo van.

The woman glanced in the back but the Cowl was playing possum. He needed all the information he could get from these two and sometimes simply being quiet was the way to go.

"The Toymaker wants him out of the way before he puts his plan into action tomorrow night," she explained slowly, as if to a dullard "He says if anyone could mess it up, it's that guy." She used her thumb to point to the Cowl.

Ralph rubbed his jaw. "Well, I can tell you that guy has one hell of a right hook."

So the Toymaker was about to do something and it was going to happen the next night. The Cowl had heard of the Toymaker but so far the man had kept a low profile. Other than a few bank jobs, the criminal had been mostly small time. Now it appeared, the Toymaker was going for something bigger.

Ralph remained silent from then on, and as the cargo van left the city and headed for the outskirts, The Cowl knew it was time to act.

Pulling his legs up, he craned his hands as far as they would go. An average man wouldn't have been able to contort to reach his boot, but the Cowl had trained with yoga instructors and could move his body and shift it in ways that had taken years to master.

His index finger could just reach the top of his left boot, and after a full minute of stretching, he was able to press the hidden button there. A knife handle popped out, the spring engaged, and he carefully used his index and middle finger to slide the blade free of the boot. It fell to the floor of the van but there was so much noise that neither Ralph nor the woman heard it.

He scooted down some more and picked up the blade, then proceeded to cut his bonds. The ropes came away easy, no match for the razor-sharp blade.

In one smooth movement he got to his knees, then his feet, and having to duck so as not to hit his head on the van ceiling, he lunged at the driver, backhanding Ralph in the face. The driver cried out, startled, and the van swerved across the highway, other cars beeping in fury.

The woman let out a curse and pulled a gun from a jacket pocket, but the Cowl slapped it out of her hand. It fell to the floor and slid into the back of the van, rattling the entire way. Yelling with rage, the woman tried to grab him but the Cowl slapped her in the face. Her ears rang and she slumped back in her seat, dazed.

Ralph punched the Cowl in the side of the body, and the blow caused him to hesitate and catch his breath. The punch had been right in the solar plexus, and even the Kevlar in the suit hadn't stopped the full force of the impact.

As the Cowl paused, Ralph reached out and grabbed him by the back of the neck, then slammed the Cowl's head into the dashboard.

Still weak from the knockout gas, the Cowl went face first into the dash, but managed to turn his head to the side at the last minute. He was spared a broken nose from the action.

Yanking his head free, the Cowl pushed back so that he was almost sitting on the lap of the woman, who was coming to and was trying to shove him off her. Meanwhile, the van was careening across the highway, cutting other vehicles off and making more than one of them crash. Headlights flashed from other cars as they tried to get the van to pull over.

This had to end soon, the Cowl knew, so taking a chance, he lunged for the driver but instead of attacking, he leaned over Ralph's lap and pulled the handle on the door. It opened and began to swing back and forth. The muscular man wasn't wearing his seatbelt, which made the Cowl's next move all the more easier.

The Cowl pushed back on the woman and her seat, ignoring her punches, which he barely felt thanks to his suit. He raised his feet and pressed the soles tight against Ralph's hip, then kicked out with all his might.

Ralph let out a yelp, and though he tried to hold on to the steering wheel, his lower body flew out into the night.

The Cowl lowered his legs and slid into the driver's seat, then pried a screaming Ralph's hands off the steering wheel. As the last finger let go, Ralph let out one last scream that seared the night, then he was bouncing behind the cargo van and rolling like a toy ball. Cars screeched and honked horns as other vehicles tried to avoid running over the man who had suddenly appeared in the middle of the highway. A pickup truck lost that fight and Ralph's body was lost under the pickup to be crushed under the undercarriage.

After gaining control of the van, the Cowl looked at the woman in the passenger seat. She was staring at him, her mouth curled into a sneer.

"Once we get off this highway, you're going to tell me all about this Toymaker and what his plans are," he said, his voice hard.

She laughed. "Oh, you think so, do you? Please, there's nothing you can do or say that would make me talk to you. Do you know what the Toymaker would do to me if I did? Trust me; it's far worse than anything you could think of."

He slowly turned his head so he was looking directly at her. "Wanna bet?" There was just a hint of a smile on his lips, and upon seeing it, her complexion went pale. He saw that she knew he meant what he said. "You'll talk to me all right. I'm not the police. I don't play by the same rules as them."

She looked frightened now, but there was something there that said she wasn't terrified of him, but what the Toymaker would do to her if she talked.

As if to solidify his assumptions, she suddenly opened her door, her hair whipping around her beautiful face from the wind, and before the Cowl could tell her to stop, grab or pull her back inside the vehicle, she rolled out of the van while it was going over sixty miles an hour. The last thing he saw of her was that she was smiling, smug in the fact that she was denying him the chance to interrogate her.

He hit the brakes and pulled over to the side of the highway, horns blaring at him in anger as he did so, but by the time he stopped she was so far behind him he couldn't even see her body in the rearview mirror. He did see the headlight's of cars swerving and crashing however.

Sirens could be heard, coming to aid all of the accidents. Punching the steering wheel in anger and frustration, he sat there for another full minute. Then, deciding there was no point in staying, and not wanting to talk to the police who were very much *not* in support of his vigilante justice, he pulled back onto the highway and drove on. He found a turnoff, took it, and got on the opposite side of the highway, then aimed the front bumper of the cargo van back to the city.

He barely glanced to the left when he passed the scenes of the accidents, ambulances and fire trucks having already arrived to help anyone in distress, and to peel Ralph and the woman off the pavement.

Whatever was going to happen tomorrow night was no doubt going to be big if the Toymaker went to so much trouble to capture him. The Cowl hated having to wait and find out what was coming with the rest of the city, though the city had no idea of what its coming fate might be. But whatever it was, he would be ready…or so he hoped.

The next evening just before sunset, the Cowl heard of the first sign of the trouble to come on the police scanner as he sat in his lair, brooding and going over the mistakes he'd made the previous night.

"Attention all units, multiple reports of…" The dispatcher on the scanner hesitated. "Multiple reports of a sighting of a giant robot in the downtown area. All available units please respond."

On one side of the lair there was a wall of televisions, news from all over the state as well as international news, playing twenty-four hours a day. A few seconds after the dispatcher had put out the call, all the local TV channels went live to downtown where there was a three-story tall robot standing in the middle of street.

Traffic had stopped to a standstill as horns honked loudly, and people either ran away screaming or stood still, gawking up at the giant robot in amazement. Fire trucks and police squad cars were already on scene, their lights strobing brightly as night began to fall.

The robot had a cylindrical body with three digit hands that were more like clamps than fingers. The entire hands on both sides were painted a dark red, like gloves. The head was wide and oval with a mouth painted on it with white teeth and red lips. There was a face painted there too, that looked like white pancake makeup. The Cowl realized the face resembled a clown's face, right down to the bright red nose that protruded from the center of the face. The nose alone was half the size of a Honda Civic

Then all the screens flickered in the lair and went to static, to be replaced by a logo of a giant teddy bear holding a model airplane. The words, **Toys are Fun!** were below the logo.

The Cowl sat up straighter in his chair. Upon seeing the toy logo, he put two and two together. He was about to get his first glimpse of the infamous Toymaker, yet another in a long line of costumed criminals that had been popping up in the city as of late.

The logo disappeared to be replaced by what the Cowl at first glimpse thought was a boy with a sagging face, but then he realized that the boy was an adult who suffered from Progeria, which was a disease that produced rapid aging beginning in childhood.

"People of our fair city," the Toymaker said, his hands held out before him, as if he was embracing the masses. His voice was high and the Cowl had an image in his mind of one of the Lollipop kids from the *Wizard of Oz*. "I am the Toymaker. By now I'm sure you've seen my mechanical behemoth standing on Broadway. As you may assume from my name, I love toys. As a man who never got to grow up, you could say that I'm obsessed with them. But I'm also obsessed with money, so if the city officials don't pay me ten million dollars by dawn tomorrow, I'll burn this city to the ground and take what I want from its ashes. To prove I'm serious, I'll be giving a demonstration of my power in exactly thirty minutes, so anyone who doesn't want to die might want to get far away from my lovable robot." The screen flickered and returned to the toy logo, to then be replaced by the news channels live in downtown as the Toymaker released control of the airwaves back to its owners.

The Cowl sighed heavily and stood up. "Here we go again," he said under his breath. Turning, he went off to the part of his lair housing his mini-jet plane. He would need something small to maneuver through the skyscrapers of downtown.

The jet was the size of a 1979 Cadillac, the finish dark black. Most of the weight of the machine consisted of the twin jet propulsion engines. After the design had been perfected, the schematics had been sold to the U.S. Air Force through one of the Cowl's many companies. He'd made millions on the deal, but the plans had been invented in the first place only because of his private battle against injustice

"Open," he said, and the voice-activated cockpit popped open with a hiss of hydraulics. Climbing in, he began flipping switches and going through the pre-flight check as the engines surged to life and began cycling for take off. Huge suction vents began taking the exhaust from the small room the jet was housed in and expelling it outside.

Minutes later, the jet began to rise, then hovered six feet off the ground. Landing gear retracted next and with a burst of fire from the engines, it shot forward into the dark tunnel before it. The Cowl's face glowed red from the illumination of the instrument panel as he piloted the sleek craft through the maze of underground tunnels that led to the outside from a hidden egress built into the side of a mountain—a mountain he owned.

Once outside in the open air, the Cowl banked upwards, gaining elevation, then pushed the throttle forward, the jet taking flight to soar high above the clouds.

Glancing at the glowing displays on the instrument panel, he found the one that had the time. It was close to the deadline the Toymaker had given the city. The Cowl didn't know what sort of demonstration the Toymaker had in mind but if he had a three-story robot to do it, it couldn't be good.

He would arrive at downtown just a few minutes after the deadline. A black-gloved hand reached out and flicked a switch on the panel and a monitor came on with one of the local news stations.

"I'm standing here in downtown, Marsha," the announcer said to the anchorwoman back at the station. "The police have cordoned off the area around the giant robot and all nearby buildings for a block in radius have been evacuated. Where I'm standing now is as close as they'll allow any news crews." The man had the generic look of most reporters, with black hair styled perfectly and makeup on his face so he looked like a mannequin more than a human being. He wore a three-piece suit under a long overcoat. "Wait, something's happening," the reporter said as he looked behind him to see why everyone in the crowd of onlookers standing around him had begun to call out and yell, many pointing at the robot framed in the camera behind him. "The robot is moving, Marsha, I repeat, the robot is moving."

The screen changed to the news station, and on Marsha, a twenty-something blonde bombshell that looked like she should be walking down a runway in her skin-tight red dress, not delivering the news. "Do you know what it's doing, Mark?" she asked, excitement in her voice.

The scene went back to Mark the reporter and stayed there. "No, Marsha, not yet. It appears to be turning a little." This was apparent to anyone watching but reporters loved to state the obvious and Mark was no different.

The giant robot finished turning and it raised its claw-like hands high over its head. Then with one mighty step that shook the ground and set off car alarms of cars parked around it, the mechanical monster moved closer to the office building it was facing. Its foot came down on a blue Toyota, flattening it to a pancake. Multiple colored fluids dripped out from under the foot from the squashed car, like it had been an animal run over by a car.

When the arms came down into the side of the building, spraying concrete and glass in all directions for half a block, it felt to anyone watching like the earth was coming to an end. Smoke billowed out from the damage and people began to scream and many tried to run. Some were knocked over, where they were promptly crushed to death as others in their panic stepped on them. Chaos reigned in the street as the police began to open fire on the robot, the bullets ricocheting off the metal skin and not so much as leaving a scuff on its shiny surface.

When the smoke and dust began to clear, it showed that a large section of the office building was missing. But the robot wasn't finished. It started pounding on the building again and again, then started moving around the structure, hacking away at the cement-coated steel pylons that were the supports. The building was over fifty stories tall, relatively a small structure in the city but still a large building. The robot punched over and over, moving around the entire building until it ended up where it started. The building looked like a tree that had been chopped on all sides as a woodsman had gone around it, the third story all but destroyed.

Then the inevitable happened. With nothing to support the building but its center, it began to topple, the minute amount of the third floor not enough to hold up the building. The fourth floor suddenly came crashing down onto the second, and above the fourth floor, the rest of the building had no choice but to follow. The weight of it all made the entire building fall into itself, as if someone had been planning on demolition and knew exactly where to set the charges. With smoke ten stories high rolling across the street in both directions, the dust cloud poured into adjoining streets, causing panic and car crashes in all directions. The entire downtown area was thrown into total chaos. People were dying in the hundreds from pure panic alone.

The Cowl saw all this on the screen before the picture went dark as the smoke cloud enveloped the reporter and the cameraman.

But he had seen enough. The Toymaker had to be stopped before he destroyed the entire city. He knew there would be no payment of ten million dollars, for if the city capitulated to what was basically a terrorist threat, then even more costumed crazies would appear for their piece of the pie. The city had to refuse, no matter what the cost.

At least with the chaos the robot had wrought, there would be fewer civilians in the area, so the Cowl knew he wouldn't have to hold back in the battle against the robot.

"Arm missiles," the Cowl said as he soared above the clouds. Estimation to downtown was five more minutes. His jaw was taut, and if he hadn't been wearing his gloves, his knuckles would have shown white as he gripped the controls of the jet.

The Cowl was confident he was ready for whatever the Toymaker could throw at him.

As the Cowl descended from the clouds to see what was left of downtown with his on board cameras, two police helicopters circled the robot, snipers hanging out of open side doors and firing at it.

The robot could have ignored the choppers, as they were nothing more than a nuisance, like a mosquito to a giant, but the Toymaker wanted to make his point that he was not to be 'toyed' with.

The robot's torso swiveled around on its waist so that the upper portion was facing behind it, then the machine raised its right hand. Just behind the claws a rectangular hatch slid open and a .30 caliber machine gun popped up. An instant later, the air was filled with the sound of machine gun fire as the robot sprayed the two helicopters. The heavy rounds penetrated the frames of the choppers with ease, slicing them to ribbons before hitting something vital. The choppers went down a few streets over, lost from sight behind the skyscrapers, but the twin fireballs that rose into the night a few seconds later told that both aircraft had gone down hard. The Cowl hoped no innocent bystanders had been hurt from the two crashes. There were probably injuries though. In a city of millions, there always was.

Suddenly the radio receiver in the cockpit of the jet crackled to life. The Cowl always had the radio set on automatic, keyed to pick up certain names, phrases and call signs from the police and military. So when the Cowl's name was broadcast, the dial immediately settled on the frequency.

"Ah, the Cowl I presume. I was wondering when you'd show up," the Toymaker said, his voice higher thanks to the speakers in the jet cockpit. "So much for my plan to dispose of you beforehand. But no matter, my giant robot is more than a match for you and your fabled toys. In fact, though I have to admit you do have some wonderful toys, I'm afraid mine are so much better."

"Surrender now and I promise you'll be treated well," the Cowl said, speaking normally, the audio receiver in the cockpit relaying his words into the transmitter and to the Toymaker.

There was a reply of high-pitched laughter, then a *tssssking* noise. "I don't think so, Cowl. The only thing I'll be accepting is my ten million dollars." There was a pause. "And your death."

The nose on the robot began to move away from the face; it tilted back so that the nostrils were horizontal. There was a loud *whoosh* sound as two SAM (surface-to-air) missiles streaked out of their launching tubes.

Alarms began to sound in the cockpit and the Cowl glanced at a radar display. The words **Incoming Projectiles: Take Evasive Action!** flashed prominently across the screen.

Slamming the thrusters hard, the jet shot forward as the two SAMS flew upward and before leveling off upon picking up the jet's heat signature.

The jet had no armor; it couldn't have any, as it was lightweight. If it had been armored than the propulsion system would have had to be twice the size. The jet was more for stealth though it did have offense capabilities. Two Mohawk (air-to-surface) missiles were hanging from the bottom of the aircraft, and there was a small gun cannon on the nose.

As the Cowl took evasive action, he deployed countermeasures. The small, fast-burning flares were made to give off maximum heat.

But neither SAM was taking the bait and they zeroed in on the jet. Diving straight down, the Cowl flew into the manmade canyons of the city, zooming past buildings only a few feet from his wings on either side. The SAMS dove downward and followed, locked onto the jet's heat signature. The game of cat and mouse was on, and if the Cowl made one wrong move, he would either be blown up by a missile or would crash and burn after hitting a building. People looked up as a small jet zoomed by overhead, the wind made by its passing sucking up the trash and debris that a city created on a daily basis. Newspapers flew everywhere, fluttering in the wind.

The instrument panel was going crazy, alarms sounding in an effort to get the Cowl to return to the sky where the jet belonged. With potential impact sites all around, the jet's computer was in chaos. No pilot should ever be trying what the Cowl was doing, but then, desperate times called for desperate measures.

Neon lights on building facades flashed past the cockpit as the Cowl flew down another street, the bottom of the aircraft only a foot from a semi sitting in traffic.

The SAMS were getting closer, and he knew he needed to take a chance or it would be over soon.

Banking to the right, he flew into the financial district, the jet weaving back and forth as it flew down streets at breakneck speed.

The SAMs were still on his tail.

Then he made his move. Banking to the right, he flew straight at a building still in construction, only the steel skeleton having been built. With everything going on in the city today, the site was empty, the foreman sending the men home for the day.

The Cowl aimed the nose of the jet directly at the building. His on board computer was working overtime as it crunched numbers. Checking his display, the Cowl saw the SAMS were right behind him. He soared into the building, the wing tips missing steel girders by inches.

Swerving and weaving, he did it all manually. He was moving too fast for even the computer to process a flight plan through the maze of steel. The jet jerked straight up and the Cowl began flying vertically as he soared up what would be an elevator shaft when the structure was finished. The first SAM followed smoothly. But the second missile wasn't able to correct for the sudden change in direction, and it went straight instead of curving upwards. It struck a steel girder and exploded into a blazing fireball.

His lips set tight in a grimace, the Cowl saw the explosion in his rearview camera, but knew he wasn't out of the woods yet. He still had one more to deal with.

Soaring out of the building, he banked back towards downtown. Maybe he could use the missile against its owner, and make the SAM strike the robot. It was risky but worth the shot.

The SAM was close now, and no matter how he zigged or zagged, it was right there.

"Are you having fun playing tag with my toys, Cowl?" the Toymaker asked. "It looks like it's about to be over I'm afraid. My missile is about to catch you and then you'll be 'it.' But you won't just be 'it', you'll be dead." High-pitched laughter sounded and the Cowl flicked a switch, turning off the speaker.

One more glance at his instruments told him that no matter what he did, he wasn't going to lose the SAM, so he banked to the right and began losing altitude. He'd set up his route back to downtown so that the robot would be facing him. Diving into the concrete canyon that was downtown, he aimed the nose of the jet directly at the chest of the robot.

"Oh ho, what's this?" the Toymaker asked from within the head of the robot as the Cowl's jet banked low and began flying right at him. "It appears the caped fool is going to ram us." He laughed yet again. "I wonder if he knows that the armor of this robot is far too thick for him to do any damage. Ah well, let him find out for himself."

The instrument panel was a glowing mass of lights, alarms sounding everywhere. The Cowl tuned it all out as he armed the two Tomahawk missiles hanging from the undercarriage of the jet, and with one last glance at the SAM on his tail, seeing it was seconds away from impact on one of his engines, he pressed the 'eject' button on the cockpit.

One second alarms bells were sounding, and the next air was rushing in and the night was all around him. The Cowl soared up and over the robot's head as the jet impacted on its chest. The Tomahawk missiles exploded on impact, as did the jet, which was a missile on its own. A fraction of a second after that, the SAM struck the fireball blossoming on the robot's chest.

The Cowl saw none of this as he flew through the air like a runaway missile himself. At first he was nothing but a dark object moving without control, but then he disengaged from the cockpit chair, and as he went one way and the chair the other, he opened his cape to catch the wind. The cockpit chair flew straight into an office building, shattering the window before rolling through ten cubicles until stopping. People not evacuated screamed as they ran from the projectile.

Miraculously, no one was hurt. The Cowl soared to the left, avoiding the building, and came down on a parked car that already had shattered windows from the force of the blast when the building the robot destroyed came down.

He landed hard and for a few seconds he simply laid there, as all around him onlookers gathered and pointed at the man in a black suit and cape who had just fallen out of the sky, while many took pictures with cell phones.

The Cowl heard the unmistakable voices of police officers as they made people move out of the way. But by the time the three officers reached the car where the Cowl was, there was a cloud of smoke, and as it dispersed, all that remained was the impression his body had made in the roof—the Cowl was already gone.

The Cowl had used a smoke pellet to mask his movement. He'd pulled his grappling hook from his utility belt, and as he laid on the car, he'd shot the line straight up at the building rooftop above him.

Then he was being pulled upwards as the grappling gun's small motor wound the line back up.

His body was sore but he hadn't broken anything, his battle suit saving him from any real harm. He began running from roof to roof, so he could return to the robot. If he had calculated correctly, there would be nothing left of the robot but a pile of scrap metal.

When he arrived over the street looking down on the robot, he found that he was half right. There was still a large black cloud of smoke from the explosion and fires were burning everywhere. All the surrounding buildings with windows that hadn't been broken when the other building had come down were now shattered from the shockwave of the multiple explosions.

Downtown looked like a war zone, with nothing but crushed vehicles, pieces of cement and glass, as well as insulation and office furniture from the fallen building, and all the debris that was created when the contents of it was smashed on the street like a broken egg.

Sirens wailed in all directions as the city services tried to maintain order. As the smoke began to dissipate in the night air, the devastation of the explosions from the jet, its two missiles, and the SAM began to show itself.

The robot was destroyed, with its arms and legs having been blown off in the blast. The torso was nothing but smoking wreckage, and off to the right, lying on its side, was the head of the robot.

Other than a small hole about two feet in diameter over the painted left eye, the head seemed intact. Sparks flickered in the hole from severed electrical wires and hydraulics, but that was it.

The Cowl was about to relax and sit down on the roof, satisfied that the job was done, when the head suddenly shifted and landed so that the clown face was level with the ground instead of on its side.

Through a loudspeaker mounted in the head, the Toymaker said, "It seemed I miscalculated the magnitude of the explosion. Indeed, my robot's armor wasn't enough. I applaud you for your ingenuity, Cowl. On the next robot I'll make sure to remedy that situation, I assure you. But no matter, this head is still more than enough to get me paid—and kill you."

The head began to shake slightly, then like it was right out of a cartoon of transforming robots, hatches began retracting and arms and legs grew, while armaments popped out of the top. The limbs were thin, insect like, and on the end of the arms were dual machine guns instead of hands.

The painted grinning clown face seemed all the more eerie now that it was a body all by itself. The head was double the size of a Sherman tank and was still more than a formidable enemy, to the Cowl and the city.

"Peek a boo, I see you," the Toymaker said through the loudspeaker, then the arms swiveled in the Cowl's direction and began firing.

The Cowl was taken completely off guard, and as he stood on the edge of the roof, he suddenly found it unstable as the bullets chewed away at the concrete beneath his feet. He found himself falling a moment later.

Instinct took over in an instant and the Cowl used his grappling gun to shoot a line to a building across the street. With pieces of the roof crashing into the ground, the Cowl wasn't mixed in with the debris, but was swinging across the street.

The Toymaker was ready however, and the guns swiveled and shot at the place the grappling gun was attached. As the Cowl swung across, he suddenly found his line had gone slack and he was falling again.

He managed to twist so that he landed on his shoulder, coming down heavy on the hood of a car that was already all but flattened from falling debris.

The machine guns had shifted from shooting the grappling line, and inexorably the rounds struck the side of the building, and as they crept closer to where the Cowl had fallen, it was only seconds before he was riddled with bullets, even his battle suit not enough to handle the steel-jacketed bullets.

The Cowl was dazed, and though he fought to shake free of his fugue, he knew he wouldn't be able to in time.

He rolled off the hood of the car, landing hard on the ground. It was funny; the three feet to the ground from the hood was far more painful than the fall when the line was cut.

No doubt he'd broken something this time. When he tried to move his left arm and right leg, both flared with agony that went up and down his body like a lightning bolt. The limbs had either been broken or dislocated. All he knew was that it hurt like hell.

The bullets were still coming down the building, leaving giant gashes in the stone in their wake. He crawled back a little so that his body was pressed up against the passenger seat of the car, hoping to use it to shield his body from the bullets. A second later, the first round struck the front fender…and went right through it as if the car had been made of paper.

The Toymaker was using armor-piercing rounds. His battle suit wouldn't be able to stand up to those. The rounds wouldn't just kill him, they would tear him up until there would be nothing but bloody pieces.

He was out of ideas, out of options. He couldn't run away, he couldn't fight with a broken arm and leg. There was nothing else he could do. All he could do was wait and die.

But before the bullets reached him, the firing ceased, and after the powerful reports, the street seemed to be almost quiet, despite the wailing sirens and screams coming from nearby streets.

"I must admit, Cowl, I'd believed you to be a much more formidable adversary," the Toymaker's voice boomed through the loudspeaker in the head, the clown face grinning with what now seemed to be pure malevolence. "But still, you did break my toy so I guess you deserve points for that. But the game is over, and sorry for you, but I win. Goodbye, Cowl."

The machine guns began firing again, chewing up the car from the front fender, the bullets working their way down to where the Cowl sat hunched over.

The engine was no match for the armor-piercing bullets either, the rounds punching through it as if the motor was nothing more than tissue paper. It was painfully obvious that the Toymaker was having fun, playing with the Cowl as the ending came.

The bullets were inches from the Cowl, and he waited to feel the first one punch though his body, feel the numbness that came with a catastrophic gunshot as the blood seeped out of his body to fill the inside of his suit.

But then there was a sound joining the machine gun reports, a soft *whoosh* that came from just behind where the Cowl was hiding. An instant later there came an explosion and the guns ceased, and suddenly metal pieces of the head began to rain down around the Cowl. All he could do was press himself against the car and pray nothing big landed on him.

A massive blast of heat washed over the car, the very air being sucked out from the vacuum.

The Cowl activated the oxygen in his mask and mercifully, air filled his lungs a split-second later. All he could do was wait for the worst of the blast to subside, and when it had stopped raining metal fragments, he struggled to his feet, though he had to use the car for support.

He was so weak he couldn't have fought off a baby if he'd been forced to, but luckily there was no one to fight. The clown head was gone, destroyed.

Later, he would see news footage of what had happened. A LAW rocket had been fired directly into the gaping hole of an eye on the head, the hole there from when the robot had been blown up.

Though the head was armored, the inside was not, and the rocket had exploded within the head, which in turn had destroyed it utterly. All that was left of the Toymaker himself was bloody gobbets of flesh that dripped down the sides of the nearby buildings still standing.

As the Cowl stood up and stared at the destroyed head, not understanding what had happened, footsteps sounded from behind him, as the owner crushed glass and rubble under his feet.

Turning slowly, The Cowl saw a strange sight in the middle of the devastation that was once downtown. It was a clown, complete with white face, red nose and lips, and bright blue hair.

The clown wore a yellow and blue outfit with red buttons down the middle. Big red shoes with bells on them were on the clown's feet and he carried a LAW rocket tube minus the rocket, which had just been fired.

There was a big white plastic flower on the right breast of the clown. He walked up to the Cowl and said, "You look like you could use a drink, friend," in a jovial voice. Then the flower squirted water into the Cowl's face, who could only sputter and step back a little. If this clown had wanted to kill him, there would have been very little he could have done to defend himself.

"Who are you?" the Cowl asked while shaking his head to clear the water from his face. Sirens were getting closer. Now that the robot was destroyed, the authorities would be moving in. The Cowl knew he needed to be gone before that happened.

In reply, the clown did a spin kick—the bells ringing happily on the foot—that struck the Cowl in the chest, sending him flying backwards to land on a pile of debris. A rock dug into his back even through his suit and he let out a brief bark of pain. He laid there, too weak to move, his hurt arm and leg screaming at him as bursts of pain filled him from head to toe. It was all he could do not to pass out.

"The name's Clownface," the clown said happily. "Clowning is my shtick. The Toymaker crossed a line with the face painted on that mechanical man of his. No one does clowns without my permission." He leaned forward so that he could better see the Cowl's eyes. "This city's mine now, cape boy, and the next time we meet, I won't be so accommodating. But I want you at your peak before I take you down, not lying in the street like a wounded dog." The clown tossed the Cowl a business card that landed on his chest, then pulled out a horn from a pocket like on a child's bike and squeezed it twice. *Honk-honk* wafted out into the night air. Then he waddled off down an alley and was gone.

The Cowl shifted position and picked up the business card with his good hand and read:

CLOWNFACE
For All Your Crime And Party Needs
Jokes Can Kill
555-DEAD

The Cowl slipped the card into his utility belt and shakily got to his feet. Picking up a piece of rebar about four feet long, he used it like a cane and began hobbling away. The sirens were loud, on the edge of the devastation, and the first responders were even now running to where the Cowl was. He hobbled into another alley than the one Clownface had taken, found a manhole cover, and dropped down into the sewer. By the time the police reached the alley, the Cowl was gone, lost in the sewers beneath the city.

It would be a hard trek back to his lair but he would make it, and once he'd recovered, he would give Clownface a call.

They had unfinished business to discuss.

THE RISE OF CLOWNFACE

Located on the outskirts of the ever-growing city were the dockyards. During the day, the docks were a bustling sprawl of business and workmen, all seeing to the import and export of items in and out of the city. Everything from toilet paper to toy dolls came in through the docks. But with so much merchandise in one place, corruption was sure to follow in one form or another.

On the very edge of the dockyard, the west side facing the harbor so that the brick wall was no more than ten feet from the stone wall of the dock, was a dilapidated warehouse, one that should have been torn down years ago.

Almost all the glass of the building had been broken, thanks to punks using them for target practice in the wee hours of the night. Crackheads called the building home, as well as more than a few homeless people.

But tonight the building was devoid of its usual residents, all having been cleared out at gunpoint hours earlier by small-necked thugs with automatics. Those that wouldn't go easily were beaten to within an inch of their life, to then be driven to the edge of the dockyard, where they could crawl away to sleep somewhere else or perhaps die where they lay. To the thugs, it didn't matter one way or the other.

When the last vagrant was rousted and the building was empty, the first new visitor stepped inside the warehouse. He was the orchestrator of the emptying of the building. He gazed around at the graffiti-covered walls, broken glass and discarded remains of a thousand take-out meals, and a look of disgust crossed his face. He pulled a handkerchief from his pocket and raised it to his nose to hide the smell of human urine and feces.

He glanced down at his shoes, making sure there was nothing on them, that he hadn't stepped in anything as he entered the warehouse. He was dressed in a pinstripe suit, a black fedora covering his balding pate. There was a bulge under his left breast lapel, where a chrome-plated pistol rested in a shoulder rig. But the fedora covered something else as well. It hid from view the large steel plate embedded in his forehead and the top of his skull. Taking off his hat, he held it in his hand, twirling it by the brim absentmindedly.

A group of six thugs were waiting for the man in a corner of the warehouse, smoking and talking amongst themselves. With the warehouse cleared of anything human, their job was done temporarily. One of the thugs, a particularly gorilla-looking gent, walked over to the man and stopped when the new arrival was standing before him.

"All set, Steelplate," the thug said. "The place is yours."

"Good," Steelplate said, his Brooklyn accent so heavy it was as if his words were slurred. The moonlight filtering into the large, open space of the warehouse reflected off the polished steel plate in his head as if it was mirrored glass. The origin of the plate was a mystery, even to the crime boss' trusted henchmen. All they knew was that Steelplate had come to the city from the east and had set up shop, a crime syndicate that rivaled the Mafia in New York.

Rumors flew about who Steelplate really was, the most popular being that the man had left New York to escape from another crime boss he'd worked for after Steelplate had stolen over two millions dollars in gold and cash from him.

Once he'd set up his operation here, that crime boss had sent his best killers to take out Steelplate. The rumor was that Steelplate had sent the hired killers packing back to the Big Apple, but only their severed heads had made the journey back to New York. After that, New York had left Steelplate alone, deciding it wasn't worth trying to kill him.

"Have the men spread out and guard the perimeter, the rest of our invitees should be here shortly," Steelplate said as he walked around the warehouse, inspecting it. "And get me a damn chair I can sit in that won't get my suit dirty."

Two hours later, Steelplate stood at the head of a makeshift table, his army of thugs standing behind him.

The table was nothing but an old piece of plywood with cement blocks for support, but it served him well for what he needed it for. On three sides of the table, a few feet from it, were small construction lights so that there was illumination. The warehouse's electricity hadn't worked in years, and each light was connected to a car battery.

At the opposite end of the table, stood another man with five thugs of his own. This man had a thin face and a sharp nose, his chin almost nonexistent. Thin, wiry hairs poked out of his cheeks, just like whiskers. He went by the name Ratface because of his resemblance to the infamous rodent. He was also the main crime boss for the south side of town.

To the left of Ratface stood another man. But this man was the exact opposite in looks to Ratface.

Where Ratface was long and skinny, the man dubbed Musclehead was a powerhouse of squat muscle, with hands the size of hams and broad shoulders to match. Musclehead ran the north side of town, everything from prostitution to drugs to gambling. Behind him stood three of his own men, each wearing wife beater tank tops and arms rippling with muscles. All three men plus their boss had pistols tucked into the waistband of their pants.

On the right side of Ratface was one more man. Covered from head to toe with knives of all assortments, many of them for throwing, the man known as Blade stood still and silent. Even his eyes didn't move, but despite this, there was a catlike quality, as if the man was ready to pounce at a split-second's notice. He had no thugs with him, confident he could kill anyone who tried to do the same to him. He ran the east side and also the docks, where the meeting was taking place.

That left the west side of the city to Steelplate, who ran it with an iron fist; one as hard as the one in his skull.

Steelplate's eyes played over each of the other crime bosses of the city and he nodded, satisfied that all but one of the invitees had accepted his invitation. The missing man was of no consequence anyway. The missing man was someone who had just popped up in the city and so far had been pulling bank jobs and jewelry heists. But Steelplate knew there was a reason for this. The new player in town was gathering finances so he could take a bigger piece of the pie down the road. No matter, that person would be dealt with in due time if they became an actual rival.

Steelplate stood as tall as his five foot eight inch frame would allow. "Gentleman, thank you for coming tonight. We have much to discuss."

"Oh yeah? Like what?" Ratface asked, his whiskers twitching like his namesake. The other men in the room nodded and mumbled ascent.

Steelplate held out his hands as if to appease his audience. "Please, please, hear me out. For too long have we been fighting amongst ourselves. I hit Ratface's men, he hits Blade's people, who then go after Musclehead's rackets and then he tries to take a couple of blocks on my side of town. Round and round we go, whacking each other's guys but not making any money."

"So what're you sayin'?" Musclehead asked.

Steelplate slammed his hands on the plywood table. "I'm sayin' that we need to consolidate our businesses. If we join forces we could own this entire town. No one could touch us. We'd be kings of the city."

"Sounds like a lot of bullshit talk ta me," Musclehead said, cracking his knuckles, the sound so loud it made some of the thugs behind Ratface jump and their hands slide closer to their weapons.

"It's not just talk," Steelplate replied. "It can be fact. Listen, gentlemen, it's not enough to just be a criminal, we need to be men with vision, artists if you will. With myself as your leader, I can make us a league to be feared by the public, but not just feared — respected, too." He raised his hands above his head, as if he was addressing a massive crowd instead of only three crime bosses. "No one would be able to stop us! Not the police, not the military, no one!"

"You forgot about me," a cold, hard voice said from above, the owner lost in the shadows of the rafters, where the lights didn't reach.

All eyes turned upward to see who had spoken, to see who would be foolish enough to invade a meeting of the crime bosses of the sprawling metropolis.

Steelplate gazed upward as well, his hand already reaching for his gun, while the others did the same, so that in mere seconds there was an army of men, all bristling with weapons. Blade pulled two throwing knives off his chest and held one in each hand.

"Who dares to come here?" Steelplate demanded. "Show yourself now or die like the fool you are." The warning was for nothing. The instant the owner of the voice showed himself, Steelplate planned on killing the intruder anyway.

Suddenly, from the shadows in the rafters another shadow appeared, moving out of the darkness and into the light. For the space of a heartbeat, no one moved or breathed, all eyes on the dark, mysterious figure looming over them.

"The Cowl?" Ratface yelled, breaking the silence. "What the hell is he doing here, Steelplate? You said this meeting was a secret."

"It was. I mean it is," Steelplate responded. He looked to his thugs, then at the other crime bosses. "Well, don't just stand there gawking like idiots. Kill him!"

Before the words had left his mouth, the sound of gunshots echoed throughout the warehouse as all the crime bosses and their men began firing.

But the space the Cowl had been occupying was already empty, the bullets striking the ceiling of the warehouse. As the Cowl dropped down from the rafters, he tossed a smoke pellet before him. A large smoke cloud erupted amongst the shooting men at the same instant that the Cowl dropped down onto the makeshift table. The wood wasn't strong enough to take the impact and it cracked in half, the Cowl anticipating this and rolling off the table in a ball and across the floor.

He jumped up after three rolls, pulling a Cowlarang at the same time. He knew he had to keep moving, and as he darted to the side, bullets churned up the concrete where his feet once were. He threw the 'rang at the first thug he saw, the sharp tip of the 'rang embedding itself in the thug's wrist, causing the man to drop his gun. The Cowl was right behind the 'rang, and as the thug cried out in pain, he was sent sprawling a heartbeat later by a blow to the chin that sent the man crumpling to the floor, unconscious.

"What's the matter with you guys?" Steelplate screamed. "Shoot him already!"

"We're tryin' boss, but he won't stay still," one of Steelplate's thugs replied as he shot at the Cowl but continually missed. The figure in black was like a wraith, always moving, never still.

Reaching into his utility belt, the Cowl pulled out another pellet, this one filled with tear gas. Throwing it into the center of Ratface and Musclehead's men, the thugs immediately began coughing and hacking. Four of the men shot each other as they tried to see. The bodies slid to the floor, the men bleeding out, unaware they'd been shot by friendly fire.

Three more men were quickly tied up using a 'rang with a nylon cord attached to it. Wrapping around the thugs upper bodies, they were entangled so tightly they could barely move. Then one of them miss-stepped and the trio fell to the floor in a tangle of limbs. The Cowl raced over to them and knocked each one out with a blow to the back of the head.

More gunshots sounded within the smoke cloud hanging in the air. The Cowl felt three punches to his chest and one to his side as the bullets struck him. Though the Kevlar-lined suit protected him from serious harm, no doubt there would be bruises there; red and blue welts to add to the many scars on his body already.

Darting to the left, the Cowl went to a steel pylon that supported the ceiling, hiding behind it as more bullets ricocheted all around him, zipping through the air like angry hornets. Once more reaching to his utility belt, he pulled a small flash bang grenade and tossed it where he believed the bullets had originated. Seconds later, there was a flash of bright light and a loud pop, followed by men yelling and screaming.

The second the grenade went off, he was already in motion, dashing across the warehouse and plunging directly into the group of thugs, who were holding their eyes and ears as they struggled to deal with the after-effects of the grenade. The Cowl was a blur of motion as he punched, kicked and punched again, taking down one thug after another, none of them understanding what was happening as each of them fell into unconsciousness.

Ratface, who had been hiding behind a crate, jumped up and began to run for the door, wanting to make a hasty exit. Upon seeing this, the Cowl pulled another 'rang from his belt, this one with a heavy lead tip. Measuring distance and the speed needed to make the throw in the blink of an eye, he threw the 'rang at the retreating Ratface, striking the thin man in the back of the head. Falling face first, Ratface landed on the cold cement floor like a lead weight himself, out cold from the blow to his skull, blood seeping from his nose after hitting the hard concrete floor.

Just as the 'rang had left the Cowl's hand, he found himself grabbed from behind by Musclehead.

"I have you now, little man," Musclehead laughed. "I'm gonna crush you like the bug you are." He began squeezing his arms together, compressing his prisoner's chest so that the Cowl began wheezing from the pressure.

Spots of light began dancing past the Cowl's vision as he felt the life being squeezed out of him. He had only seconds left before it would be too late to fight the powerful man off. His arms were pressed tightly to his sides by the crushing grip of Musclehead but the Cowl managed to shift his left arm an inch to the side so he could use his fingers and pull one of his Cowlarangs from his utility belt. He came close to dropping it as Musclehead added more pressure, but with sheer determination, the Cowl twisted the 'rang in his hand and jabbed the sharp tip into Musclehead's leg. The brute howled as the steel tip pierced his flesh, and though he didn't let go entirely, the grip on the Cowl lessened slightly.

That was all the Cowl needed to make his escape.

Yanking his right arm free and over his head, then his left, the Cowl reached back and clapped his hands together hard. His guess was right and his hands slapped Musclehead's ears, causing the large man to howl again and this time let the Cowl go as he brought his ham-sized hands up to his ears, which were ringing painfully.

Dropping to the floor, the Cowl sucked in air as he fought off a wave of dizziness. If he fainted now there would be no waking up.

Sweeping his right leg out, he hooked his ankle around Musclehead's left leg and sent the man crashing to the floor. Then, before the large crime boss could get up, the Cowl pulled a small pellet from his belt and squeezed it under Musclehead's nose. The sleeping gas took immediate effect, the large thug passing out a second later.

Taking a quick look around the warehouse, the Cowl saw that almost all the thugs were down and out for the count. But Steelplate was nowhere to be found.

However, before the Cowl could do a search for the crime boss, Blade stepped out from around a pile of boxes, the knives on his chest glistening in the two remaining construction lamps still working.

"Bet you think you're tough," Blade hissed. "Well, you haven't had to deal with me yet." At the end of his sentence, two knives flashed in the air as he flicked them at the Cowl.

Dodging to the right, the knives sliced the air, but missed the Cowl completely. He had no more than moved when two more knives came at him, the deadly accuracy of Blade uncanny. The Cowl used his wrists to block them, the Kevlar deflecting them easily. But the knives had been going right for his lower face, the only exposed area on his body.

The Cowl immediately realized this man was a formidable match in skill and could do with knives what most men did with bullets. He knew within a heartbeat that the only way to take down Blade would be up close and personal.

With more knives flashing at him, the Cowl rolled and jumped, coming up only a few feet from Blade. As he did, he pulled two Cowlarangs from his utility belt, holding one in each hand.

"Ah, so you want to play, huh?" Blade hissed. "Fine, let's see who the better swordsman is." As if by magic, two short swords appeared in Blade's hands, each no longer than a foot. The handles were made of brass with small jewels encrusted in the hilt. From the way the man held the two weapons, the Cowl had an idea they meant something to the swordsman.

"Don't say much, do you," Blade said as he attacked. "Want to be the strong, silent type, huh? That's fine with me. Silent, talkative, they all die the same in the end."

The Cowl blocked the attack, his 'rangs deflecting the small swords. The air filled with the clanging of the two men as they fought to the death. To anyone watching, the battle was a blur of steel ringing on steel, the metal flashing in the glare of the light lamps. Blade knew when to attack and when to defend and the Cowl knew they were both evenly matched. For the next five minutes, the battle raged on with neither man getting the upper hand. One advantage the Cowl had was his Kevlar suit, something Blade was severely lacking. Then Blade managed to slip by the Cowl's guard, but the tip of the sword only rebounded off the Cowl's suit, the movement throwing off Blade's attack.

The Cowl took the moment of hesitation, something measured in microseconds, and lunged forward, his right-hand 'rang slicing across Blade's abdomen. There was a tearing sound like wet parchment being ripped, and an instant later, Blade was standing immobile, looking down at his intestines as they pushed forth from the incision across his stomach. His mouth fell open in amazement and he dropped the short swords, his hands going to his guts to try and push them back in.

"I...I don't understand," he whispered. "I didn't win. But I always win, I'm the best." He slumped to his knees as he looked up at the Cowl. "I can't die."

The Cowl went to the man and helped Blade lay down. "I didn't mean for this to happen, I only meant to wound you." He paused. "Stay still," the Cowl said. "I've already called the police on this meeting, they should be here soon. Paramedics will be arriving as well. You'll be okay, you can live through this; you just have to hang on." As if to punctuate his words, sirens could be heard wailing in the distance. There was still time before the authorities arrived but they were on the way. Just before he'd shown himself, the Cowl had called the police anonymously to let them know there was a meeting of the major crime bosses of the city.

There was a lot of blood mixed in with Blade's guts and the Cowl realized something major had been cut as well. The man was bleeding out. The Cowl, desperate to save Blade, plunged his right hand into the wound to try and find the bleeder, but with his gloves on his fingers weren't sensitive enough to feel around. Retracting his blood-soaked hand, he prepared to take the glove off and try again, but when he glanced at Blade's face, he saw that the man was already dead. The swordsman's eyes were open and glassy, staring at the ceiling high above. The mouth hung slack and there was no movement. Placing two fingers behind Blade's left ear, the Cowl found no pulse.

The Cowl was on his knees and he slumped back on his haunches, staring at the dead man before him. He hadn't meant to kill Blade, and never would have even tried. One of his vows as the Cowl was to never take a life with his own hands, but now before him was a dead criminal, the life taken by his hands.

The sound of a shoe coming down on spent shell casings floated in the still air of the warehouse. The Cowl spun around and rolled to the side just as Steelplate fired his handgun, the bullet missing the Cowl's face by an inch. The man had been hiding behind a pile of empty crates, and upon seeing the Cowl hunched over Blade, he took the opportunity to finally kill the Cowl.

The Cowl came up in a rolling jump and dashed around the warehouse as Steelplate fired round after round, only hitting air. When Steelplate's gun clicked on an empty chamber, the Cowl darted in and knocked the empty gun from Steelplate's hand with a closed fist, then punched the crime boss in the jaw, sending him reeling backwards to land on an old wooden crate. The crate splintered from the weight of the thug and Steelplate found himself trapped, his butt wedged in good.

"You're finished, Steelplate," the Cowl growled. "You're going to jail for the atrocities you've committed here and in the past across the city."

Steelplate began to laugh, and he let his body go limp, as if he was relaxing inside the crate. "We'll see about that, Cowl. I have a damn good lawyer. I'll be out in time for dinner." He laughed even harder. "And when I tell the law I'll cooperate and pinch you for the murder of Blade, I'll be sitting on easy street in no time."

"That was self-defense," the Cowl hissed. "I didn't mean to kill him."

Laughing so hard that the crime boss began to turn red, he said, "Tell it to the law, killer. I know what I saw." He stopped laughing abruptly, his face totally serious. "But if you let me walk right now I could be persuaded not to say a thing. It could be our little secret. So what do you say…" He paused. "Killer?" He said the word as if it was something to be proud of.

"Never. I'll gladly go to jail if it means getting scum like you off the street," the Cowl replied, his bloody right hand squeezed tightly into a fist.

Steelplate shrugged. "Suits me. Be a martyr, not that anyone will care or know."

"I'll know!" The Cowl screamed in frustration. He'd killed a man and no matter how he spun it in his head if he tried, the end result would always be the same. He regained his composure, deciding the night could still be salvaged if he could get the information he needed. "Tell me about Clownface. I heard he was going to be here tonight."

Steelplate shrugged casually, his demeanor light, as if they— criminal and superhero—were sitting in some cozy bar having a drink together, talking about old times. "He didn't show up, not that I care. A freak in a costume, how dangerous could he be? I merely invited him for a laugh. Figured the boys would get a kick out of some sideshow nutjob. I mean, who dresses up in a costume and runs around the city; am I right or what?"

The Cowl growled low in his throat, then curled his hands into even tighter fists and stepped forward

Steelplate raised his hands in surrender. "I mean other than you, of course. Not you, you're a man to be reckoned with, I know that now." Another pause, then, "Killer." The nickname was said to be hurtful. When the Cowl winced at the word Steelplate knew he'd hit a nerve.

So Clownface hadn't come and the Cowl's main reason for breaking up the crime meeting had failed. Well, not entirely. All of the four major crime bosses were down for the count, one put down forever, something the Cowl would have to wrestle with for many a day. With the other crime bosses in jail, the city would breathe easier for a few months, that is until the next in succession came up the line and took over for the jailed crime bosses. There were always more; take one down and three more criminals would pop up to replace the one eliminated.

The sirens were getting closer, only minutes away. The Cowl knew it was time to go. He would deal with the fallout of Blade's death later. He went to Steelplate and pulled the man from the crate. The thug actually tried to take a swing at him, but the Cowl blocked it easily and punched Steelplate in the kidney, making the crime boss keel over, wheezing. "You can't blame a guy for tryin'," he said, expelling air heavily.

The Cowl spun him around and pulled a zip tie from his utility belt, then secured the crime boss' hands. He would hang Steelplate from one of the rafters before he departed the scene, where he would await the arrival of the police. Glancing around, all the bodies on the floor were still, either unconscious or having been killed by friendly fire. That wasn't something he felt guilty for. If one thug shoots another, it was hardly his fault.

He was about to shoot a grappling line to one of the rafters and hang the crime boss up, when suddenly a door at the far end of the warehouse opened a few inches and a red-gloved hand poked through, then tossed a bright red ball ringed with circus animals into the warehouse. The ball rolled across the floor, missing all the bodies and debris scattered about until it stopped only a few feet from where the Cowl stood. The Cowl, the ball, along with Steelplate, were actually almost dead center of the bodies strewn across the floor.

There came a crackling hissing sound from overhead, and the Cowl glanced up to see hidden speakers mounted on three of the rafters. He had seen them when doing recon of the warehouse earlier, but hadn't given them much thought, assuming they were part of the original building. The speakers' outer shell had been camouflaged with dirt and grime to make them look as old as the building, though they were brand new, and the electrical wires powering them had been hidden as well.

"So, Cowl, we meet again," a voice said through the speakers, echoing across the warehouse. The voice was male but with the distortion from the speakers that was all the Cowl could discern.

"Who are you? Show yourself," the Cowl said; he was searching the warehouse with his eyes but he could see no sign of the owner of the hidden voice.

"Sorry, cape boy, I assumed you already knew who I was. Need a hint?"

The Cowl's eyes creased in anger. He knew who was talking now, thanks to the name 'cape boy' the hidden speaker used.

"Clownface," the Cowl said matter-of-factly.

"In the flesh, so to speak. See that ball there? Of course you do. Well, it's full of C4; more than enough to blow up the entire warehouse and everything inside it. See, when Steelplate got word to me that he was holding a meeting and I was invited, well, I couldn't simply arrive and barter for my piece of the pie. Oh no. Why not take the whole pie instead. Hell, why not take the kitchen the pie was made in and the farm the fruit was grown on, too? So I've been waiting to blow all the crime bosses sky high so that I can pick up the pieces. I told you before this city would be mine, and after I blow up this warehouse and remove the competition, it will be. But then there's you. Which was why I've waited to blow everyone up. I must say you put on quite a show and I simply had to see if one of those goons was going to be the death of you. Blade had a chance but you showed him, didn't you. My, my, but we are a bloodthirsty little cape boy, aren't we."

"That was an accident, Blade wasn't supposed to die," the Cowl said.

Steelplate had been listening the entire time and now said, "Listen, Clownface, if that's really you talking. We can work out a deal here. Sixty-forty, we can rule the city, just you and me."

"Cape boy, I suggest you shut that goon up or I'll press the button right now and we can end our conversation sooner rather than later."

"Huh? What's he talkin' about?" Steelplate asked but the Cowl moved up to Steelplate and karate chopped him on the back of the head, knocking the man unconscious.

"Good, much better, now we can finish our chat," Clownface said over the speakers. The Cowl began searching for a hidden camera somewhere in the rafters or on one of the walls of the building, knowing there had to be one somewhere for Clownface to know what was going on the same time it was happening.

"You're getting cold, cape boy, no, wait, now you're getting hot, hotter, ah now you're cold again," Clownface said as the Cowl moved around the warehouse searching for the camera. Considering the camera could have been the size of a small button, the odds of finding it by the eye alone was all but impossible.

"I warned you that the next time we met I wouldn't be so accommodating," Clownface said. "Though I have to admit that I thought our next meeting would have been more, hmm, what word should I use. Ah, I have it—dramatic. But we don't always get what we want in this world now do we. So I guess I'll have to settle for blowing you up with the rest of the dirtbags. Ah well, see you in that big carnival in the sky, cape boy. Bye-bye."

The bomb began ticking, each tick getting higher in pitch. At the same time the ball began to expand, doubling in size with each passing second. The Cowl could see he had seconds before the bomb exploded, incinerating everything within the warehouse.

His eyes darted to all the bodies on the floor, especially the ones like Musclehead and Steelplate who were unconsciousness, but he knew there was no way to save them and himself as well. He had to be selfish, or he would end up dying in a blazing inferno along with his enemies.

Turning, he pulled his grappling gun and shot a line up to a rafter near the windows facing the water. The line zipped through the air and the metal hook wrapped around a rafter, then he was being pulled up into the air.

"Hey, where do you think you're going?" Clownface asked from the speakers. "There's no escape, you know, all the doors have been sealed. But don't worry, it'll be over in a few seconds."

The Cowl ignored Clownface's taunts, instead focusing on swinging upwards and to the side. His feet connected with the window first, the plate glass exploding outward in all directions. His Kevlar suit protected him from harm, and he made sure to cover his face with his arms as he burst through the window. Just before he crashed into the plate glass, he heard Clownface say, "Why you clever little…ah well, maybe this is for the best. Until next time, cape boy." Then the bomb exploded and the world became nothing but bright light and heat as the Cowl found himself plummeting to water, thrown sideways by the shockwave of the explosion. Instead of a controlled landing in the water, he fell upside down, and as he entered the harbor his cape became tangled around his head. He began struggling to fight free of the cape, as the water pulled him ever downward.

He found his breath already exhausted, and with his arms tangled in his cape, he couldn't reach his utility belt to grab an oxygen canister with a small valve on the end to put in his mouth. The rebreather was still in its testing phase, and when it was done, it would be sold to the military for millions for use by SEAL teams. The Cowl had one now but it was as if it was a million miles away with his hands constrained.

The darkness swallowed him whole as he sank ever deeper, and though he felt his consciousness slipping away, he fought to the last second, never giving up, his indomitable will not allowing him to—and then it happened.

His right hand found a tear in his cape. It must have happened with his fight with Blade. Shoving his fingers into the tear, he yanked down hard, making it bigger. Soon his entire head was through it, then his shoulders. With his arms free, he shimmied down the cape like it was a dress, and with the cape attached to him by one side, now more like a giant streamer than his faithful cape, he began swimming now that he was disentangled.

His lungs were ready to burst, his mouth ready to open and take in what his body assumed would be air, but instead would be the filthy water of the harbor. He could imagine the feeling as the cold water filled his chest, causing him to choke and gag as his lungs were saturated with water.

His vision was going and his mind started to grow foggy, but still his arms reached for the surface, his legs kicking as hard as he could.

Then just when he opened his mouth, unable to stop his body from doing what it wanted, what it needed, his head burst free of the surface and instead of sucking in water he sucked in the cool night air. There was the tang of ash and wood smoke in the air but despite this, that first lungful was the best one he'd ever taken in his life.

He floated for a few seconds, just breathing, thankful he was alive and not becoming a bloated corpse at the bottom of the harbor. Before him was what remained of the warehouse. It was almost complete rubble, with only the north wall still standing. The rubble was ablaze, the oranges and reds licking skyward. Police and fire services were already on the scene, but there was nothing any of them could do but watch the conflagration.

The Cowl set off for the far side of the dock, where he then climbed out of the water and used an adjacent building to the one near the fire to block him from view. As he came out of the harbor and his feet touched dry ground, the first thing he did was pull off his cape, then wrapped it into a ball and tucked it under his arm. It was ruined, tatters now, and would only hinder his escape.

When he was sure it was safe, he slipped off into the shadows of the night, to a building two blocks away at the edge of the dockyard. His dark sedan was waiting, the car hidden in a building owned by one of his many corporations.

As he made his way through the night, careful not to be spotted by anyone, he thought about the past hour and how once more Clownface had gotten the better of him.

The first time had been with the Toymaker, and now with Steelplate, but the Cowl vowed that the next time they met, the Clown of crime wouldn't be as lucky.

Blade's body had been incinerated in the explosion, so there would be no way to tie the corpse to the Cowl, but still, the deed had been done, the Cowl had taken a life with his own two hands, and though Steelplate was dead and couldn't blackmail him for Blade's death, as were the other crime bosses and their thugs, Clownface was still alive and knew what he'd done.

The Cowl had to wonder if the killer clown had a video recording of the deed, as the warehouse had been wired for picture and sound.

The Cowl knew too well that he'd crossed a line this night, killing Blade in what was self-defense but to the Cowl felt like a murder. The Cowl was a skilled fighter, thanks to years of martial arts training, and though Blade had been good, in the end the Cowl would have prevailed. He never should have sliced Blade like that; he'd expected the man to move backwards but instead Blade had stepped forward, right into the razor-sharp 'rang.

The Cowl should have foreseen such a move, he should have remained in control to the very end of the fight, but in the heat of the moment he'd lost control.

He'd killed one of his enemies, the one thing he'd sworn he would never do upon first donning the mask of the Cowl.

The question on his mind now was: would the line between not taking life be forever erased? The next time he was in a similar situation, would he react in the same manner? Would he be able to go back to the way things were?

One thing was for sure; the Cowl and Clownface would meet again, and when that time came, one of them would fall.

TO CATCH A CLOWN

The trap door in the floor opened without warning, sending the Cowl spinning into darkness.

His reflexes being close to superhuman, he instinctively pulled his grappling gun and shot a rappel line up into the ceiling to prevent his descent, but as he fell, the twin doors slammed closed above him, snapping the line and causing him to tumble into the darkness once more. Reaching out, his hands felt protuberances along the wall—some were vents, others were extended pipes— but he couldn't get a grip on anything, as if the objects had been coated in grease; which unknown to him they had been to prevent him from halting his fall.

Despite not being able to get a good grip, each time he tried to hold onto one such object, it would still halt his descent slightly so that instead of plummeting to his death, he fell more slowly. When the last object had been grabbed and lost, he found himself spinning in the air, and he had just enough time to get his head tucked under his arm, moving his body so that his armor-covered shoulder took the brunt of the landing, which came far too quickly for his liking.

Grunting with the impact, the Cowl saw flashes of light across his vision as the breath was knocked out of him. He sprawled across the cold concrete floor, his head groggy from the impact, and he fought the urge to slide into unconsciousness.

It was pitch black, not to so much as a flicker of light coming in through the now-closed trap door incredibly high overhead. He lay on the floor, staring upwards, knowing he needed to get up, to face whatever danger was coming for him. Because there had to be a threat, or else he never would have wound up in the trap he now found himself in.

For a few brief seconds, the Cowl lay prone on the floor, his mind flashing back to how he'd arrived in his present predicament.

Since his fateful meeting with Clownface at the warehouse two weeks ago, where the Cowl had barely managed to escape with his life, he'd been searching for the whereabouts of Clownface's hideout. The harlequin of terror had been suspiciously quiet since then, as if he too knew to show himself would mean that the Cowl would be on to him.

Over time the Cowl had managed to acquire a few snitches in the criminal underbelly of the city, men who would sell their grandmothers for a dollar. These men had kept their ears to the street, listening for any mention of the name *Clownface*.

And then, a day ago, the Cowl was contacted by one of his snitches, and upon meeting the man, had received the information he'd been so desperately waiting for.

The location of Clownface's hideout.

The snitch had been paid handsomely, and the Cowl had quickly done his research on the supposed location. He wasn't so foolish as to just go rushing in without checking the place out first. Clownface may have been insane, but the villain was also crafty, and nothing was ever as it appeared.

The building was in the factory district, and when the Cowl began digging through his computer files, he found that the building was owned by a shell company that was owned by another and so on.

The Cowl had continued digging until discovering the final name of the holding company that was above all others.

It was called 'Bigtop Incorporated.'

Instantly, the name reminded the Cowl of a circus, and what were in circuses but clowns.

The name of the company was Clownface showing his hand, for the evil clown was a narcissist and couldn't help himself. No doubt it was part of his sickness, and whatever made him do the evil things he did, that same thing would be his undoing.

So finally, the Cowl had finally found Clownface's lair.

That night the Cowl set off to do a little recon, but when he found the building deserted, he couldn't help himself and had entered through an open skylight. His helicopter was a block over, sitting silently on a dark rooftop.

Attaching a line to the edge of the skylight, he'd dropped into the darkness below, the line playing out to allow him to slide down it. Touching down silently, he found himself in an office-type setup, complete with cubicles filled with office furniture.

Nothing out of the ordinary, here, so he continued searching, floor by floor, until he reached the basement. Here, things didn't seem to be as 'normal' as the floors above.

The basement seemed unused, filled with long corridors of stone, and pipes overhead, the metal steaming incessantly. Wary of a trap, he'd gone deeper into the sublevel, until coming to a long corridor that seemed to lead somewhere of interest. The clues were the posters of clowns on the walls, one after another. If this wasn't a breadcrumb trail to what was down here, the Cowl didn't know what was. The question was: were the posters there for him or for someone else?

That was when the floor seemed to evaporate and the Cowl found himself plummeting into emptiness.

His brief recall ended as soon as it began when a maniacal laughter sounded throughout the darkness. Next the darkness was banished, as recessed spotlights flashed on; the light was so bright it would have blinded the Cowl if not for the lens filters he wore over his eyes. The filters were all but overloaded, however, the illumination of such a high intensity.

The laughter ceased and a man's voice said, "Well, hello there, killer. It's so nice of you to 'drop' by." The laughter began again, the voice finding the little pun incredibly amusing. "But you won't be here long, I assure you. In fact, very soon you'll be a dead man."

"Clownface, so it's you," the Cowl hissed.

"Of course it's me, you black-caped fool. Who else would it be?"

The Cowl got to his feet, his eyes already searching for a way out of the room he now found himself in. The trap-door was high above his head and though he could shoot another line up and try to see if there was a way to force the door open, he had an idea that it wouldn't be that easy to escape. Besides, the longer he stayed, the more he would learn about Clownface and what diabolical plans the mad harlequin had up his colored sleeves.

A panel on the far wall suddenly slid open, and a view screen flicked on, and the Cowl looked upon Clownface, who was standing before the camera, in view from the waist up. In his hand was a small black box, a remote control or similar apparatus.

"Ah, there we go, now you can see me as I can see you. Isn't this cozy?" Clownface asked as he smiled his red-lipped grin at the camera.

"So what's your game this time," the Cowl asked.

"I just told you, killer," Clownface said. "I'm going to see you killed."

"You've tried before and it didn't work out the way you hoped."

"That's true, but this time I have some help." The image of Clownface faded, to be replaced by the photo of a forty-year-old man in a white lab coat, with Einstein-like hair and thick bifocals. Clownface's voice could be heard as the Cowl studied the screen, and the photo with in it. He recognized the man, but couldn't put his finger on who he was, not that he needed to.

Clownface answered the question a moment later. "Have you ever heard of medical research scientist Dr. Denton Michaels, killer?"

The name rang a bell and the Cowl quickly thought back to all he'd read about Dr. Michaels. Top of his class in every University he'd ever attended, had doctorates and Master degrees in genetics, biology, and physics, just to name a few. The man was a genius, having graduated high school at the age of twelve, and finishing his first college degree by age fifteen. But being a genius also made the young man rather anti-social, as at a young age he found others to be difficult to tolerate, because compared to him they had a limited intelligence. The scientist became a recluse, and stories of him carrying out insane and bizarre experiments having to do with everything from cloning, to gene splicing, to regrowing limbs began to surface. So much so that the authorities finally investigated him, and upon finding the rumors correct, the man was taken into custody. But not for long; the genius soon escaped, to then go deep underground so he could continue his wild and illegal experiments. The last the Cowl had heard, the authorities believed the man dead.

"I heard he was dead, caught in an explosion at a secret laboratory he had outside the city about a year ago," the Cowl stated, repeating what he'd read.

"It was all a ruse, killer. Smoke and mirrors to get the police off his trail."

"But the police found a body in the ashes."

"Yes, but it wasn't the good scientist, it was a body I ah…well, let's just say I acquired a body and that was what was found in the rubble."

"You mean you killed some innocent person and used the body to mask the doctor's disappearance."

"Potato, pot*ah*to, it's all irrelevant in the end," Clownface said. "What matters is that since then, the mad doctor has been working for me."

"Doing what?"

"Ah, killer, now that's where you come in." The Cowl had been walking around the room, trying to see if there was a way to escape. He was inspecting the TV screen when Clownface added, "Don't bother trying to find a way out, killer. There is none, I promise you that."

"I'll find a way out, Clownface, and when I do, you and me are going to finish all this once and for all."

"Brave words coming from a dead man. You see, Dr. Michaels has been busy since I took him under my wing. I've been able to supply him with everything he'd ever needed to finally bring his experiments to fruition."

"What are you talking about?"

Clownface kept right on talking, as if the Cowl had said nothing.

"And now those experiments are ready to be tested, and what better way to find out if they're as powerful as the doctor hoped, than by having them tested in battle."

Suddenly, a door slid open, revealing a long corridor that led into a maze. But the hallway wasn't empty. From what the Cowl could see before the corridor made a sharp turn to the right, every twenty feet there was a glass wall-panel that could be retracted into the ceiling. The Cowl looked down the hallway to see that behind each glass wall-panel was some kind of creature, but of such shape, size and color to be like nothing he'd ever seen before. Nothing created in Nature anyway.

"Say hello to the mad scientist's wonderful creations, Cowl." Clownface began laughing as he pressed a button, and from all three remaining walls of the room the Cowl was standing in, panels slid open to expose nozzles that began to spit fire. In an instant the room was over a hundred degrees, the temperature rising exponentially. In seconds the room would be far too hot for anything to exist, let alone the Cowl. He knew he had no choice but to exit the room—and fast.

"I thought you wanted to kill me yourself, Clownface, not have these things do it for you."

"Oh. I will. See, the monsters are just to soften you up. If you get through them all, I'll be waiting at the end, I promise." Clownface snickered. "But I highly doubt you'll make it to the end."

The Cowl barely heard Clownface, however, as he was dashing out of the room, the flames licking at his cape. Made of fireproof material, still the cape began to smolder from the shear amount of heat being applied to it. Inside his black armor, the Cowl began to sweat profusely, and though his suit was made to breathe, with the air so hot it did nothing to prevent him from practically cooking in his battle suit.

But then the Cowl was out of the room, the door slamming closed behind him, trapping him in the corridor. In front of him, the Cowl stared at the first creature he was to do battle with.

The best description of the thing was of a melding between a lizard and a man. Standing about five feet tall, the entire form of the creature was covered in thick scales. It was naked. Its long tail swung back and forth like a cat's, as if in anticipation of the coming fight. Its mouth opened slightly, and a long tongue flicked out, as if tasting the air like a snake. Its face was elongated, the jaw extended in relation to its lizard namesake. Sharp teeth were within that mouth, looking as if they could tear a man's arm off once they got a good hold. Both its hands and feet were tipped in sharp, long claws. As the lizard man moved back and forth, the claws on its feet click-clacked against the tile floor.

The two-inch thick glass wall-panel separating the Cowl from the lizard man shot up into the ceiling.

The lizard man hissed and charged at the Cowl. There was no talk, no dance, as when two men would square off after an argument in a bar. There was only the animal instinct to kill.

The Cowl dodged to the right as the lizard man came at him, but he hadn't taken the tail into account. Though the body of the lizard missed him, and its raking claws, the tail lashed out, striking the Cowl in the chest and sending him flying backwards to hit the wall and slide down it. The wind knocked out of him, he wondered if he'd broken a rib, as each time he sucked in air he felt a flash of pain in his chest.

The mutant lizard never slowed, didn't even hesitate. It spun around after missing him with its claws, and charged at him again.

Reacting as if he was battling a human opponent, the Cowl sent a flurry of punches and kicks at the lizard, but not one blow so much as slowed the creature down. The lizard plowed in, a right cross sending the Cowl back against the wall to bounce off it, before receiving yet another bone-jarring blow to the chest.

The Cowl did his best to fend off the attack, but it was plain to see he wasn't going to be the victor in this duel. Reaching down, he pulled a Cowlarang from his belt and used the weapon like a knife, slashing at the lizard. The sharp tip of the 'rang only bounced off the thick scales of the creature, doing absolutely no damage.

Dropping to his knees, just as a blow swooped by overhead to crash into the wall, plaster raining down, the Cowl rolled to the side and out of the way, wanting to get some breathing room.

The lizard didn't give him the chance, and it spun around and was on him in a flash. Picking up the Cowl as if he was a child, the lizard sank its teeth into the Cowl's shoulder, the powerful jaws pressing down into the Kevlar material that made up his battle suit.

The Cowl winced, feeling the pressure of the upper row of teeth pressing down on his skin the most. If not stopped, the teeth would soon penetrate his armor. He could feel one tooth pinching his skin as it forced its way through the Kevlar.

The lizard wrapped its arms around him, and though the Cowl was almost a foot taller than the thing, the beast held the Cowl as if it was the lizard who was the taller of the two.

But the Cowl being taller still had his feet on the floor, and so with a flick of his big toe inside his boot, he activated a switch that triggered a thin blade made of surgical steel, and three inches if it popped out of the tip of his boot. Turning his foot to the side, he jammed the blade into the lizard's leg with a powerful kick. The scales were thinner here so that the lizard could have movement, and the blade slid in-between two scales just below the knee. The creature opened its mouth wide and screamed in pain—an all-too human sounding scream, far too human for the Cowl's liking—and with that the Cowl was free.

Thrusting his arms wide, he shoved himself away from the lizard man and ran to the farthest corner of the section he and the creature were trapped in, his eyes darting for a means of escape or something to use as a defensive weapon. As he went through a mental inventory of the items in his utility belt, nothing came to mind that would stop the lizard before him. No, if he was to prevail here, it would be with his mind, not his muscles.

The lizard was recovering from the wound on its leg, and though bright red blood slid down its leg to pool on the floor, it was still very active and if possible, angrier than before in wanting the Cowl dead.

The Cowl looked past the creature to see the only thing remaining in this section of corridor that was original to the building; it was mounted to the wall in a small cubby about waist height. Everything else had been stripped out. Was this a mistake, or did Clownface leave the item there to give him a fighting chance? The answer would remain unknown forever, for who knew what was in the mind of a madman.

Seeing the object as his only chance, and quickly coming up with a plan, he waited for the lizard to attack him again, and when it did, he sidestepped the creature, then used his clasped hands like a bludgeon to punch the lizard where he believed its kidney would be, before making a mad dash across the corridor to the object on the wall.

Shattering the glass, he yanked out the fire hose within.

Hissing in anger, the lizard man had already spun around and was charging at him again. The beast was relentless, and the Cowl had a feeling in the end the lizard man would win out by sheer indefatigable strength alone.

The Cowl waited until the last second before moving this time, the lizard man, with its head low like a bull, coming at him like a runaway freight train.

When it seemed like the creature was going to plow into the Cowl, he darted to the right, spinning back around to face his foe, the fire hose coming up like a lasso. Wrapping the hose around the lizard man's neck, the beast hissed in anger, but the Cowl was too fast to be stopped. Before the lizard man could do anything, the hose had been wrapped around its neck and the Cowl yanked back, pulling the lizard to the floor, where the Cowl then jumped onto its back and wrapped the flaccid hose around its neck yet again, making a double loop. Then he dashed to the small red valve that turned on the water, filling the hose with high-pressure liquid.

The lizard was trying to get free of the fire hose, but the hose was wrapped too tight around its neck. The water began to flow, filling the hose, stretching it, the makeshift noose around its head growing ever tighter.

Pressure was beginning to build as the noose grew even tighter. The lizard man's eyes began to bulge out of their sockets, its mouth opening wide, the tongue sticking out to wave in the air.

The Cowl could see it wouldn't be long now.

Staggering back and forth, the lizard man clawed at the hose, slices appearing in the thick material from the beast's talons. Water shot out of the jagged tears but the hose was still mostly intact, the pressure continuing. If the creature had had more time, it no doubt would have been able to slash the fire hose to shreds, and thus free itself. But time had run out, and the hose squeezed so tight that the lizard man's head simply *popped* off, the severed head flying straight up to hit the ceiling before falling back to the floor. The Cowl was reminded of the cork from a champagne bottle being released, only here no one was cheering when the cork had popped.

Blood shot out of the neck opening of the lizard like a water fountain, small and large spurts of crimson dancing in the air as the headless beast stumbled back and forth, its hands reaching up to the empty air where its head was supposed to be.

The hose, now free of its wrapping, untwisted, flying around the corridor like a living creature, a snake that had finally broken free of its prison. The Cowl had to duck down or else risk being struck in the head with the flailing steel nozzle. With the hose end whipping around like a thing gone mad, the Cowl rushed to the valve and quickly turned off the water.

The hose slowed and dropped to the floor, now limp and still, the water trickling out of the slices in the material.

Letting out the breath he was holding, and wincing at his hurt ribs, the Cowl let his shoulders sag slightly as he slid to the floor, relaxing slightly, knowing the danger was past.

"Not bad, killer. You got lucky," a familiar voice said from hidden speakers in the ceiling. "But you're not done yet. Four more to go before you reach me. One of them will take you out eventually."

Before the Cowl could reply, the next glass wall-panel slid up, letting the mutant waiting within out.

"No rest for the wicked and all that," Clownface laughed, as the mutant came charging forward, directly at the Cowl, who was already getting to his feet.

This mutant resembled a frog, but was the size and shape of a man. The mix of human and amphibian DNA had left the skin a weird purple color, as if the melding of green and flesh tone had made an entirely new pigment. It stood no more than four feet tall but the mass of its body was compact and solid muscle.

Its ears were large, the lips thick and fat; the similarities to a bullfrog staggering. Its hands and feet were webbed, and gills could be seen on its neck, though the mutant also breathed air. The eyes were large and round.

The Cowl had just gotten to his feet when the frog thing reached him. An arm came up and around, batting the Cowl like he was made of paper, sending him flying across the corridor to bounce off the wall.

Though the air was forced from his lungs, the Cowl managed to pull a Cowlarang and throw it at the creature. This 'rang had an explosive tip, and the plan was to simply blow the creature up, then he could use another explosive 'rang and try and break himself free.

Just before the 'rang went off, the frog thing knocked it from the air, sending it spinning to impact with the wall. The shock-wave of the blast was enough to stagger the mutant though, and when the dust cleared, the Cowl saw that behind the plaster the wall was solid cement blocks. He wouldn't be using explosives to escape anytime soon, at least not with the small amount contained in his Cowlarangs.

An overhead light was shattered from the explosion, and the exposed wires began to spark and flash as the current continued to flow through them.

The Cowl looked down at the floor to see that the water from the fire hose was seeping into the next section, where the frog thing had taken up residence, and seeing this, he had an idea on how to take out his next foe.

The frog man charged at him, its short legs pumping like a lo-comotive, its webbed feet slapping the floor and causing the entire corridor to shake. It was such a solid mass of flesh and muscle that the Cowl knew there would be no way to win with only his fists. The mutant only wore a pair of red shorts that stretched to conform to its body. Seeing a bulge at the junction of its legs, the Cowl realized that the mad doctor who had created this thing had done too good a job in melding human and amphibian.

The amphibian ran straight for him, and when it was only a few feet away, the Cowl ran at it as well, and just before they met, he spun around, sweeping his right leg in an arc, the leg horizontal to the floor, the sole of his boot even with the frog mutant's crotch.

Running far too fast to stop, the amphibian plowed directly into the extended foot. The Cowl felt the testicles of the creature implode beneath his heel, then the frog man crumpled up, screaming at the top of its lungs. The scream, however, got higher in pitch with each passing second. The Cowl had made a falsetto of the thing.

"Oooh, that's gotta hurt," the Clownface said from hidden speakers, causing the Cowl to grin as he darted around the immobilized creature. He then reached up to where the sparking wires from the light still sizzled.

Though the ceiling was only a few feet above him, he pulled his grappling gun and shot it straight up, then secured the line to his belt. Reaching up to a pair of sparking wires, he yanked them hard, pulling them out of the ceiling, but not so hard that they didn't stay connected to their power source. Then he pulled on the grappling line and was raised off the floor, which was still covered in water from the torn fire hose.

The amphibian was recovering slowly, the pain subsiding slightly, despite the damage to its groin, but the Cowl didn't give the frog man anymore time to gather its wits. As the creature began to get up, the Cowl leaned as close as he dared and touched the sparking wires to the thing's shoulders, one on each side.

The Cowl's gloves were insulated, but the frog man was not, and as it was standing in water, the mutant's entire body began to twitch and shake, the muscles locking up as volts of electricity surged through it from head to toe.

The smell of cooking meat filled the air, the distinct odor of frog's legs being fried in oil coming to mind. Boils erupted on the frog man's arms and legs, as the body was burned from the inside out, and a silent scream escaped the misshapen mouth. The eyes began to melt, and the strange-color skin began to slough off its bones.

Smoke began seeping out the mutant's ears, and as if a timer had gone off, signifying that the amphibian was done, the head exploded, the internal pressure too much for the cranium to hold.

The Cowl let go of the wires, letting them fall to swing back and forth, still sparking and hissing like living things. The frog man stood perfectly still, though minus its head, then the body topped forward and splashed into the water coating the floor. The water did little to put out the smoking corpse.

The Cowl dropped down onto the floor as well, safe as long as he stayed clear of the sparking wires.

The sound of snickering came from the hidden speakers. "It smells good in there. Frog legs anyone?" Clownface quipped, laughing heartily as the amphibian settled into the inch high water across the floor. "What, nothing to say, killer?"

"What do you want me to say?" the Cowl asked.

"Oh, I don't know; you could tell me how you're going to make me pay when you reach me. That is, if you somehow manage to take out the other three of the good scientist's creations."

That made the Cowl look down the long corridor at the three remaining creatures trapped behind the thick wall-panels of glass.

"Somehow I think your luck will run out eventually," Clownface pressed a button and the next glass wall-panel slid up, freeing the waiting mutant. "Next!" the harlequin of evil yelled, his hysterical laughter fading away before ceasing entirely when the speaker cut off.

The Cowl heard none of this, as he was already focused on the charging behemoth coming at him like a runaway freight train.

The mutant was a melding of rhino and man, the large horn protruding from its forehead looking sharp and strong enough to impale the Cowl with one swipe of its massive head. Its skin was gray, but looked tough, with dark hairs protruding along the arms and legs, as if the man part of it had been hairy.

Squat, with short, stubby legs, the rhino man practically galloped at the Cowl, its head low, the horn ready to gut him like a fish.

The Cowl could see no way to beat the mutant with brute force, so once more his mind raced to come up with a plan of attack. But for the moment, his main concern was one of defense, and as the rhino came at him, he dodged to the right at the last second, the horn on its head missing him by no more than an inch. The rhino man was going so fast that there was no way for it to stop or change direction, and it plowed right into the wall, shattering the plaster to show the cement hidden within. A thick dust cloud surrounded the creature, and the Cowl waited for it to clear so he could have another look at his foe.

Pulling a Cowlarang, he threw it at the form moving in the dust cloud. There was the sound of impact, then the 'rang flew back out of the cloud to fall onto the floor. The thing's hide was so thick that the 'rang couldn't penetrate. Unless he was lucky enough to hit an eye, there would be no way to cause damage to the beast.

The heavy footfalls of the charging rhino man filled the corridor as it came at him again. There was nowhere to go. Up wasn't an option, the ceiling only a few feet above his head; which only left moving from side to side.

Before the Cowl realized it, his back was against the next glass wall-panel.

The mutant within looked like some kind of plant monster. Humanoid in shape, but covered in a thick canopy of leaves and vines that ran up and down its body like a cardio vascular system. The swamp man banged on the glass, wanting to reach the Cowl as well.

"Wait your turn, swampy," the Cowl said under his breath.

The sound of galloping hooves, along with snorting, filled the corridor once more, the rhino man charging the Cowl like a mad bull.

Pulling a smoke pellet from his utility belt, the Cowl threw it to the floor, the cloud enveloping him almost instantly. With the distraction in place and hiding him from view, the Cowl lunged to the left, just as the rhino man came at him. Once more the beast couldn't stop, only instead of solid wall being behind where the Cowl had been, this time it was the glass wall-panel of the next mutant.

Without stopping, the rhino man plowed into the glass panel, the sheer power of the brute shattering the panel like it was made of paper, the brawn of the mutant enough to destroy the thick glass panel easily.

The swamp man instantly came forward, eager to reach the Cowl and do to him what none of the other mutants could do—kill him. Meanwhile, the rhino man had run a few more feet and was turning around to renew its attack.

Trapped behind the final glass wall-panel, a man-bat looking thing waited, hopping from side to side impatiently as it flapped its leathery wings: it wanted in on the battle as well.

Now the Cowl had to deal with two mutants at once. As the swamp man reached him, the Cowl punched it in the face, then followed up with a kick to the chest. Both blows were ineffectual, and his fist and foot actually slid into the creature's body. When he pulled them free, there was the distinct feeling and sound of suction. It reminded the Cowl of getting a foot stuck in mud and having to pull it free, the mud all the while trying to hold onto its prize.

The corridor began to shake as the rhino man charged at the Cowl again. Pieces of glass stuck to its hide, most falling off as it ran.

Moving quickly, the Cowl shoved the swamp man in front of the rhino, then jumped out of the way.

The horn on the rhino impaled the swamp man, the two mutants then moving forward, all the while the swamp man kicking its legs and swinging its arms to get free. Angry at having the wrong foe on its horn, the rhino man flicked his head to the side, and the swamp man slid off the horn and slapped the wall hard, before sliding to the floor.

The Cowl hadn't remained inactive while all this was going on, and when the rhino turned to see where the real enemy was, the Cowl dropped down from the ceiling where he'd gotten to by using his Cowlarangs like climbing tools—one in each hand—and landed on the back of the rhino man. Using one of his rappel lines, he wrapped the line around the rhino man's neck to use as a way to control the beast.

Like a bucking bull, the rhino man went crazy, but no matter how much it tried to dislodge the Cowl, the dark crusader stayed put.

The Cowl yanked on the line around the rhino's neck, and it cut into the skin—the flesh wasn't as thick here, so that the mutant could move its head easily.

Steering the rhino man towards the swamp man, once more the swamp mutant found itself impaled on the horn of the rhino, then the Cowl began steering the rhino man back to the first room the Cowl ended up in after falling through the trapdoor.

The door was closed but it was no match for the rhino man, and like a semi truck bursting through a brick wall, the mutant did the same with the door. The swamp man raised its arms to its face just before the impact with the door, then all three beings were through, the door in pieces.

The instant they entered the room once more, the panels shot open along the walls and the flames began again.

Jumping off the rhino's back, the Cowl held onto the rappel line and quickly hogtied the rhino man, then dashed out of the room as the flames licked at his cape.

Lying on its side, the rhino man couldn't move and the bonds on its legs were made in such a way that the more it struggled to get free, the tighter the knots became.

Meanwhile, the swamp man was still trapped on the rhino's horn, the weight of the rhino keeping the swamp man from getting free.

All the while the flames filled the room, making it unfit for life of any kind.

Standing at the shattered door, but a few feet more into the corridor to escape the brunt of the heat, the Cowl could see nothing within the room, the flames so thick it was impossible. But he did smell the odor of both mutants being roasted alive, as well as hear their cries of agony as they were scorched from head to toe.

Minutes later the flames ceased. But it wasn't like a switch had been flipped. It was more of a slow and steady process, as if the fuel that supplied the flames was finally exhausted.

Stepping to the doorway, the Cowl peered inside the room, his eyes immediately going to the charred corpse of the rhino man.

The only thing remaining of the swamp man was a scorched and brittle skeleton; there was also the distinct aroma of burnt flora, and a stain where the swamp man had been around the charred bones. Being more plant than man, the flames had cooked off the moisture and then the remaining moss-like substance that had been the muscle and tissue of the mutant.

The Cowl's attention once more went to the rhino man, and the horn still there. But for a few scorch marks, the horn was perfect, the bone more than tough enough to withstand the heat it had been exposed to.

Turning and peering down the long corridor, and at the man-bat thing waiting for its chance to kill him, the Cowl formulated an idea. Reaching down, he grabbed the horn with both hands and pulled it free from the blackened head. Tendons and small veins stretched like elastics as he separated the horn from its owner, the tendons finally snapping upon reaching their breaking point.

Hefting the heavy horn, he turned and left the room, walking straight down the corridor towards the final waiting mutant.

"Not bad, killer," Clownface said from the hidden speakers. "You took out two at once."

The Cowl said nothing, only continued walking towards the last remaining mutant. When he was only a few feet away the glass wall-panel slid up, letting the man-bat creature free.

But before the mutant could get more than a foot past where the wall had been, the Cowl charged it, the horn in his hands held high.

The man-bat had large wings, like its namesake, and with its arms held out wide, the wings spread apart, it blocked what light filled the corridor.

The Cowl ducked under one of the wings, coming up directly in front of the mutant, and before the thing could react, the dark crusader plunged the rhino horn into its chest, piercing its heart and killing it instantly.

Letting out a high-pitched shriek, the creature dropped to the floor, dead.

"What the…" Clownface said from the speaker, shocked to see the battle over before it had even begun.

The Cowl was already moving, however, running to the door at the end of the corridor, an EXIT sign over the doorframe. Kicking the door in with a blow from his foot, he found himself in another corridor with no doors or windows on either side, but at the far end, another door. With no other options, he began running again, while pulling a Cowlarang from his belt in anticipation of what was on the other side of the door.

Reaching the door, he kicked it in as well, and then charged inside. He rolled across the floor as he entered, in case there was someone waiting to take a shot at him, and found shelter behind a metal desk.

When nothing happened, no shots or outcries at his arrival, he popped his head up to see that he was in some kind of laboratory, complete with test tubes and other containers filled with unknown substances, many still boiling happily.

He couldn't help but become excited when he saw a colorful shape sitting behind a desk at the far end of the room. The garish wig, loud suit and red gloves told the Cowl all he needed to know—he'd found Clownface.

Going into action, he jumped to his feet and raced across the room, his right arm going back as he prepared to throw the 'rang in his hand. He was expecting Clownface to try and kill him, whether by gun or some other nefarious way, but so far the figure behind the desk was immobile.

The 'rang flew across the gap separating him from the figure, striking the body in the center of the chest. Knocked over, the colorful figure fell to the floor, the floppy red shoes flying upwards, as if the legs were stiff. So far, the figure had not made a sound, not even a grunt when being struck by the 'rang.

Now even more wary of a trap, the Cowl approached the figure slowly, but so far there was nothing amiss other than that the body appeared to be dead.

The figure had fallen onto its back, still in the chair, its arms still resting on the arm pads of the chair. But on closer inspection, the Cowl saw that the arms were actually tied to the chair.

"What the…" he said, also realizing that the figure wasn't wearing painted-on makeup but that it was a latex mask instead. Kneeling over the body, he slowly peeled the mask off the face, to expose the visage of the mad scientist who had created the terrifying experiments he'd just done battle with.

The Cowl studied the face, and the marks on the neck, a clear sign that the man had been strangled with something thin, like piano wire perhaps. The mouth was open, the swollen tongue protruding from blue-colored lips, the eyes also open and staring at nothing. It was clear the man had been dead for some time.

The Cowl stood up, not understanding why the man was lying dead at his feet. What purpose did it serve Clownface to have a corpse waiting for him to arrive?

Overhead, hidden speakers crackled with static. Clownface began to laugh. "Oh, killer, you didn't really think it would be that easy, did you?"

"I should have known you wouldn't face me like a man, you bastard. You said you'd be there waiting for me."

"I did, but I lied. I can do that, you see. I'm the bad guy after all."

Clownface slowed his laughing until it was only a few snickers. "I will face you soon enough, but only when I know I have the upper hand. You fared far better than I expected against the mad doctor's creations. I applaud you, killer. You're quite a warrior."

"Why did you kill him?"

"Ah, that's quite simply really. He'd outlived his usefulness."

"So you just killed him."

"Of course I killed him. What was I supposed to do; take him to dinner? Tsk-tsk, killer, surely you know how the game is played. I'm the villain after all. I kill people when I feel like it."

"But you didn't have to kill him, you fiend."

"Oh killer, don't act like you care so much. What's one more innocent murdered amongst friends? How many have you killed since we first met, hmmm? I know I've killed too many to count." There was the sound of a soft click, as if something had been activated, and then Clownface added, "And it's time to add one more body to my count. Farewell killer, it's been nice knowing you. This time, unlike at the warehouse, there will be no escape."

The Cowl's eyes were darting back and forth as Clownface talked, searching for an exit, or perhaps a place where Clownface might be hidden. He spotted a door at the far end of the room, with an EXIT sign over it, but whether the door led to freedom or not was something he would have to find out for himself.

Then he heard a soft beeping. Looking down, he saw a small red light flashing underneath the corpse's clown suit. Bending over, the Cowl tore open the suit to find a bomb, the countdown already down to sixty seconds. There were more than a dozen wires coming off and around the bomb, all leading off to different leads. An entire brick of C4 was wired to the detonator, more then enough to bring the entire building down on his head.

"Better move, killer, there's not much time," Clownface said, before laughing hysterically, while clapping his hands in tearful happiness.

The Cowl was about to see if he could disarm the bomb when Clownface added, "I wouldn't try to disarm it, killer. There's far too many false wires for you to figure out which one to pull in the remaining time you have left."

Knowing the evil clown was correct, the Cowl turned and dashed for the exit door. His right shoulder took the brunt of the blow when he impacted the door, forcing it inward with a spray of wood and metal from the frame.

"Sheesh, killer, it was unlocked, all you had to do was turn the knob," Clownface laughed as the Cowl found himself in a stairwell, the walls and stairs made of painted-gray concrete. "But it won't matter; you're too far underground to escape this time. You're dead, killer. *Dead!*"

As the Cowl began running up the stairs, taking them three and four at a time, he could hear Clownface's voice counting down the time.

For a few brief seconds, the Cowl was lost in his own body, only the sound of his beating heart in his ears. For if he wasn't fast enough to reach the surface, he would be buried alive by tons of debris when the bomb went off.

He didn't know how many seconds remained, and in truth it didn't matter. All that did was to keep climbing, keep moving, for to pause for even a second could spell his doom.

But though the Cowl was almost superhuman in his fighting skills, and his will was like no other man on earth, he was still only human, and eventually his time ran out.

There was little more than a dull thump when the bomb went off, for he was already many floors above the sublevel where he'd been trapped.

The stairwell began to shake and buck like it had come alive, but the Cowl still kept climbing, his hands on the railing the only thing preventing him from losing his balance and tumbling back down the stairs.

The ceiling began to crack, followed soon after by small pieces of cement tumbling to the stairs, a few pelting the Cowl's masked head. Still he moved higher, now taking the steps five at a time, his lungs working overtime to take in the necessary oxygen to keep his body moving. He was already exhausted from his previous battles, and now he had to do a sprint up countless flights of stairs.

He never thought for a second he wouldn't make it, that he would escape the tomb Clownface was trying to bury him in.

But when the lights flickered and then blinked out, plunging the stairwell into darkness, it told the Cowl that no matter how much he wanted it, and no matter how much he would fight to survive, that in the end, he wasn't going to make it.

A second before the lights went out in the stairwell, he stopped at the landing he was rounding to the next floor, and as his world began to shake uncontrollably, and even more rubble rained down on him, he lunged for the corner of the landing, and pushed himself as close to the junction of the two walls as possible. He barely managed to do this before the entire ceiling above him, and on each consecutive level, came crashing down, burying the stairwell in cement and debris.

Wrapping his body in his cape, the Cowl put his arms over his head, gritted his teeth, and pressed even closer to the wall as he was swallowed alive, enveloped in thousand upon thousands of tons of falling debris.

There was the sound of a hundred A-bombs going off in his ears as he was covered entirely, and he screamed, having to let out the pent-up panic filling him from head to toe. To die fighting in battle was one thing, but to be buried alive, trapped and unable to move, with nothing to do but wait for the air to run out, was not a way he wanted to die. Hell, he didn't want to die at all.

Like a light switch had been turned off, the explosion of noise halted, and then there was only silence, not so much as a sound being made.

The last thing the Cowl heard as he became lost in the darkness, and though it might have been his imagination, was of Clownface laughing, the evil harlequin knowing he had finally won, and had killed the Cowl at last.

The entire area was filled with the sound of work crews desperately trying to find survivors of the collapsed building, but after more than two days having passed without a soul being rescued, and due to the sheer devastation, the rescue operation had already been changed to one of salvage, for any of the bodies that might be buried in the rubble.

So far none had been discovered, and it was in everyone's hearts that no corpses would be found at all.

The halogen spotlights set up along the perimeter of the site turned the night into day. Ernie Goddowski was working on the north side of the rubble late at night on the second day, and sitting in the cab of his bulldozer, he used the rear scoop to clear away more rubble. Then he paused upon spotting a dark shape emerge from the debris, as if it was a zombie rising from its grave; to say he was shocked would have been an understatement.

The figure was dressed all in black, even a mask covering the face, only the mouth and lower jaw showing; the prominent chin told Ernie he was looking at a man. The man wore a cape, though it was nothing more than tatters now, and the entire black suit the man wore was ripped and shredded to expose the wounds beneath.

None looked fatal; merely heavy scratches and bruises, no doubt caused from climbing out of the rubble.

Over the mouth and nose of the man was a small oxygen mask made of clear plastic, and as he emerged from the rubble, he ripped off the O2 mask and tossed it and the small canister the mask was attached to onto the debris surrounding him.

For one brief moment, the man stood tall, but then he fell over and to his knees. Ernie was out of the cab and running to the man, to then drop down beside him. Ernie gave the man a bottle of water, and though the water was warm, the man drank it greedily, as if it was the coldest nectar he'd ever tasted.

"Geez, pal, where the hell did you come from?" Ernie asked. He had a hand on the guy's arm to help stabilize him and Ernie could feel that the suit the man wore was thick and heavy, like it was some kind of flexible armor. Ernie didn't know anything about Kevlar.

"The building collapsed," the Cowl whispered. To Ernie, the Cowl seemed as if he was in a daze, who only listened, nodding at each word.

This man in the dark suit of black seemed larger than life, like something out of a movie or comic book, Ernie thought. He'd heard stories on the news about some of the costumed villains running around the city, but he'd never seen them in person. In fact, he'd wondered if it was all a hoax created by the news media to boost ratings.

"I made it to a corner landing before the ceiling fell in. The walls at my back fell over too but they created a pocket for me to take cover in." The Cowl began moving out of the rubble, Ernie helping him walk.

"And you had air to breathe?" Ernie asked.

"At the beginning I did, and then it started to run out. Then I used my portable oxygen mask."

"Listen, pal, you stay here, I'll call for help."

"No, wait, don't call anyone," the Cowl said. "I managed to begin crawling upwards through the rubble. One foot at a time through any crevice I could find. Sometimes I had to dig for hours to make a hole wide enough for me to fit through. By the end of the first day I began to hear signs of work crews overhead. I called out but no one heard me—I was too far down, I guess. I slept a lot, too. It was probably from lack of clean air to breathe. I used my oxygen sparingly, knowing if it ran out before I reached fresh air I would be dead."

"Geez, pal, that's amazing. You should be dead right now," Ernie said. "But let me get you some help." He turned around and began running a few feet, rounding a massive pile of rubble, the same pile having shielded him and the Cowl from view from the other work crews.

Just before Ernie rounded the corner, he turned back to make sure the man was still there, and his eyes went wide when he saw the space the Cowl had been standing in now empty. His peripheral vision caught a flurry of movement across the lot next to the collapsed building, and he barely managed to see a dark figure before the shape vanished between two other buildings. He blinked, wondering if the shape was real or just a play of the light and shadows from the moonlight and halogen lamps.

What was real, however, was that the man he'd found emerging from the rubble was gone. A second later there was the sound of a helicopter from the other side of the building across from him. Ernie tried to see what had made the noise but it was too dark. He thought he saw a dark blur against the sky, but couldn't be sure.

He decided not to tell any of the other work crews what he'd seen this night, for without proof, they would only end up teasing him and making up jokes.

Shaking his head and wondering if he'd imagined the entire thing, he went back to work, once more searching for bodies.

As soon as the Cowl had climbed free of the rubble, and while he was with Ernie, he'd pressed a button on his utility belt, and sent a call to his helicopter, which was on the rooftop of a building a half mile away.

Inside the cockpit, the dashboard had lit up like a Christmas tree, the autopilot engaged, and the rotors began to spin. Within seconds the sleek black aircraft had risen silently into the night, to then fly off in the Cowl's direction.

By the time the Cowl had reached the corner of the next building, to be lost from sight by Ernie, the chopper was hovering overhead. He pressed another button and a thin ladder of no more than six inches wide was dropped down. Wrapping an arm around one of the rungs, he climbed onto the ladder and pressed the same button he'd used to call the ladder down. A moment later, he was being pulled up into the night sky. Even before he'd reached the aircraft, the helicopter was already soaring off to the outskirts of the city. By the time he was inside the helicopter and in the cockpit, the dark aircraft had left the city behind to be replaced by the clear glass of the ocean.

He flew out over the ocean for more than ten miles before banking back to the city, coming in on a very different flight path than the one he'd used to leave. Flying low so as not to be picked up by radar at the nearby airport, he aimed the nose of the helicopter back to his home, where he would treat his wounds, and considering the way he felt, probably sleep for a week.

After a few minutes of just flying, his mind settled a little and he was able to think back to his time battling the mutants and then his escape from Clownface yet again.

This was the second time Clownface had almost gotten him, and the Cowl knew the next time might be his last, for if the saying was true, the third time was the charm. Clownface had become his deadliest foe, a man who seemed to always be thinking one step ahead of the Cowl.

The dark crusader knew if he was to finally overcome the evil harlequin, he would have to find a way to get two steps ahead of the demon clown, or else the villain's tyranny would never end.

But that was for another time, for now, all the Cowl wanted to do was eat, shower and sleep.

So far, whenever he'd dealt with Clownface, he'd always been on the defense, but he vowed that the next time they met, the Cowl would be on offense, and finally take down the laughing harlequin, for their next confrontation would be their last, and when the time came, he vowed that only one of them would walk away alive.

THE FLAMES OF FIREBUG

With the exception of the sound of debris crunching under the Cowl's feet, only the soft drip-drip of water could be heard as the dark figure moved through the burnt-out building of what was once an office building on the west side of town. But most of the building hadn't been damaged by the actual fire; the destruction had come from the black soot that now covered everything, plus the water damage from the fire hoses that had sprayed the building with water, as well as the fire suppression system within the building, the sprinklers flooding the entire structure.

The fire had been set to make a big mess, but as long as it wasn't left alone to burn uncontrollably, the damage would be enough to condemn the building, and not make it useless to anyone who wanted to purchase it and renovate it. It was a precision burn; an arsonist had set the fire, but the Cowl needed to find proof that the fire had been set and not an accident.

However, what had brought the Cowl to this building was a curiosity. This was the fifth building in a month to catch fire, despite the structure having state-of-the-art fire suppression systems.

So far, the arson investigators had ruled all the fires accidental, but the Cowl didn't believe it. Five buildings in a month were just too much of a coincidence.

Ducking under a fallen beam blackened from the searing heat of the fire, the Cowl continued his search of the lower levels, knowing if the fire had been set, it would probably have begun in the boiler room or the space designated for maintenance, as it would have been filled with cleaning supplies, painting materials, and other flammable products.

A rumbling came from overhead, bits and pieces of the ceiling floating down to the floor, and he stopped, looking up instinctually. The building was severely damaged in this area, and he knew it was a good possibility that the wreckage above him could fall in through the ceiling of the basement. Despite himself, he cringed in panic.

Weeks ago, he'd been trapped under tons of debris thanks to Clownface, and though he wanted to think he was healed and ready for duty, deep inside his mind there was still a part of him that was now terrified of being buried alive. Only his massive will and inner strength allowed him to enter the building and go below to investigate, where a normal human would never have put himself in a similar situation.

The rumbling ceased and the building seemed to settle down—for the moment at least.

Satisfied that at least for now the danger had passed, the Cowl moved deeper into the sublevel until he reached the boiler room.

The second he entered the room, he detected the odor of an accelerant. If the arson investigator had missed the same odor he was either a fool or on someone else's payroll other than the city. The Cowl figured it was probably the latter.

He stepped on something that squished beneath his heel and he looked down to see a burned rat. The rodent was nothing but a black husk, all the hair having been burnt off it in the flames. Its eyes had exploded from the searing heat and its tongue, though a dried and brittle thing, stuck out of its mouth. The little creature had died horribly; there was no question about it. When he'd stepped on it, the rat's insides, already cooked to a well done texture, squirted out of its cracked and scorched flesh. The Cowl had seen many disgusting things over the years, some enough to drive a man mad, but there was something unsettling about this dead rat.

Sliding his boot across the floor to scrape off the burned rat, he continued onward, his small flashlight beam leading the way.

It didn't take him long to find what he believed was the origin of the fire. A number of blackened paint cans were also in the vicinity, but there should never have been anything such as paint cans in the boiler room. Just one more item he put away in the back of his mind. Studying the burn pattern, it appeared as if someone had taken a flamethrower and sprayed the walls and ceiling. Now who would carry a flamethrower into a building, let loose, and then get away undetected? Surely a man with a flamethrower on his back would be noticed fleeing the scene of a blaze.

Having collected all the evidence he thought was needed, the Cowl was about to leave when he heard the sound of footsteps coming from behind him. Turning, he saw a figure coming towards him, a flashlight in its hand leading the way.

"Hey, who's down here!" a voice called out. "This building's off limits."

The Cowl dashed to a door at the far end of the large room, moving through it silently. By the time the figure arrived at the spot where the Cowl had been standing seconds earlier, he was long gone.

Looking around and finding no trace of the intruder, the fireman scratched his head. "I could have sworn I saw someone," he said to himself. With a shake of his head to rid himself of the chill he felt at being down in the subbasement alone, he turned and got the hell out of there. His job was to make sure no one entered the building and to do spot checks to make sure there were no re-ignites from any hotspots in the rubble that might have been missed by the initial firefighters after the conflagration had been put out.

His two-way radio crackled to life and he answered it, telling the voice on the other end that he was fine and was leaving the subbasement and going to continue his search on the main floor. Spinning on his heels, he began walking back to the exit, and by the time he reached it and was heading up the stairs, he barely noticed that he was practically running.

Emerging from a hole in the wall of the first floor, the Cowl made his way around the building, where his motorcycle was waiting, hidden behind a dumpster. The bike was coated entirely in black paint, even the 1000cc engine block painted in high-temp lacquer. The machine was built for speed, with a small fairing in front to help with wind resistance.

Hopping onto the motorcycle, he flicked a hidden toggle switch under the seat, which turned on the electrical system, and a moment later the motor was surging to life, the bright halogen headlight pushing back the night.

Backing out from behind the dumpster where he'd hidden the machine, he drove down the alley and took a right onto the street, his destination his lair, where he planned to do research on the building he'd just left and the other ones that had been burned. If he looked hard enough, he was confident he would find some link to the mystery of who was doing this, whether it was for insurance reasons or some other nefarious concerns.

As he drove down the street, the few pedestrians still out this late at night watched him go by with curiosity. It wasn't everyday a motorcycle and rider, both looking as if they'd been dipped in black ink, drove through the city, and the rider with a long cape blowing out behind him.

The light at the intersection turned red just before the Cowl reached it, and he gunned the throttle, zooming through the intersection. A Corvette had taken off from its first spot in line the instant the light had turned green, and because of the Cowl basically blowing the light, the 'Vette almost hit him.

"Asshole!" the driver of the Corvette screamed as the Cowl passed his front bumper, missing it by no more than an inch.

The driver had had a very bad day and getting cut off by a motorcycle was the last straw. Swinging the car around, he began to chase after the dark motorcycle. The driver almost lost the motorcycle twice and had to push the speed limit to the max to finally reach and then overtake the bike. Pulling in front of the Cowl, the driver hit the brakes, causing the Cowl to stop or risk hitting the Corvette.

Slamming the transmission into 'park,' the driver jumped out of the car and ran at the Cowl, who was sitting on the motorcycle, watching this seemingly irate man come towards him with what seemed like amusement.

"Can I help you?" the Cowl asked with a grin. The engine on the motorcycle was still running, but it was more of a whisper than anything else, thanks to the baffles fitted into the exhaust pipes.

"Can you help me? Yeah, by letting me beat the shit out of you after you cut me off!" The driver was a tall fellow with a crewcut and heavily muscled arms.

"I cut you off? Hey, I'm sorry about that, I really am. My mind was somewhere else," the Cowl said. He wasn't going to get into specifics about how he'd been thinking about who the arsonist was, or how in the back of his mind he couldn't stop thinking about Clownface and the next time they met.

"I don't care what your excuse is, pal. I'm gonna beat some sense into you. After that you can say you're sorry and maybe I'll accept it as genuine." The driver took a step towards the Cowl, his fists raised.

The Cowl was already considering how he was going to immobilize the enraged driver. A karate chop to the throat, followed by a double-punch to the kidneys, and when the man leaned over from the blows he would finish the guy off with a final blow to the back of the neck.

It was just as he swung a leg over the motorcycle seat, so he would be standing and ready for battle, that a scream sounded from nearby. Both the Cowl and the driver turned as one, both searching for the origin of the scream, but in a city of millions, one brief scream was almost impossible to pinpoint. That is, until it came again, and the Cowl's eyes went to a dark alley on the far side of the street.

"Someone's in trouble," the Cowl said, then prepared to drive his motorcycle into the alley, as from the urgency of the scream, time was of the essence. He was about to leave when a hand clamped down on his left shoulder, the fingers locking onto him like a steel vice.

"Just where the hell do you think you're going, asshole?"

"To help who just cried out."

"No way, pal, we have business to finish here first."

Deciding time was of the essence, and not wanting to waste even a second to teach the jerk a lesson in manners, the Cowl reached down to his utility belt and pulled out a small spray bottle of some kind of aerosol. Before the driver could do anything else, the Cowl sprayed the bottle's contents right into the guy's face. The knockout gas hit the man quickly, sending him to the ground, unconscious.

Before the man was fully prone on the ground, the Cowl was already crossing multiple lanes of traffic that made up the street—blaring horns and yells of anger filling the air—and driving into the alley to save whoever needed help.

The bright halogen headlight of the motorcycle pushed back the darkness in the alley, illuminating the scene before the Cowl instantly.

There were three thugs in the alley, and they had cornered an old, married couple in their seventies, the man and woman both dressed for a night on the town. He wore a tuxedo and she a long blue dress with high heels. Around her neck was a sparkling diamond necklace and the man wore a Rolex on his left wrist. The two people couldn't have made more of a point to be mugged than if they'd both held up signs that said *"We're rich, mug us!"*

When the old man saw the motorcycle pull into the alley, he yelled, "Help us, please, they're robbing us!"

"Shut up, old man," one of the thugs snapped and punched the old man in the stomach. The old man went to his knees, wheezing, while his wife held him. "Mark, Jerry, see who that is and take care of them." The thug gestured to the motorcycle and its rider.

"Will do, Lenny," the thug named Jerry said, and then he and Mark stepped away from the old couple and ran at the motorcycle, which had now come to a stop. With the bright headlight they couldn't see the rider, but they figured they didn't really need to. Each man held a handgun in a clenched fist, and at the same time they began shooting just above the handlebars of the bike to kill the rider.

Both men waited to see the shape of the rider tumble from the seat, and when that didn't happen, they looked at one another, each man thinking the other one had an answer to what was going on.

That was when a dark shape dropped down out of the sky, as if coming from thin air, and landed directly between the two men. The Cowl's arms were outspread and he used them to halt his fall by landing on the two men's shoulders. The weight of the Cowl's body forced the thugs to the ground, each man letting out a cry of pain and surprise.

A moment before the men began firing, the Cowl had used a rappel line and zipped upwards as bullets missed his feet by inches. Then he dropped down on top of the thugs, taking them completely by surprise.

The Cowl had gone to his knees upon landing, the men taking up the rest of the impact from his fall, and he now took a step forward and turned so that as the men stood up, he was facing them.

"Where the hell did you come from?" Mark yelled, already raising his gun to shoot the Cowl.

"From your nightmares," came the reply, and before Mark could squeeze off another round, the Cowl lashed out with a furry of blows that were meant to immobilize his foe in a heartbeat.

The Cowl's first punch broke the thug's nose, dark red blood pouring down his face. The second punch shattered Mark's jaw, the lower jaw bone shattering under the Cowl's Kevlar-gloved fist. Mark dropped to the ground, gagging and spitting blood, out of the fight for the time being. The Cowl didn't take the chance he was faking, however, and he stepped forward and sent a sweeping kick into the side of the man's head, sending Mark into the oblivion of unconsciousness.

But the Cowl had looked away from Jerry for one precious second when knocking Mark out, and the second thug used that time to aim his gun at the Cowl.

As if sensing the gun being trained on him, the Cowl spun around with a sweeping kick that knocked the gun from Jerry's hand and sent it flying across the alley.

Jerry didn't let that faze him and he lunged at the Cowl, his fists pummeling the Cowl like two flesh sledgehammers. Jerry was a big man, a little over six feet, with broad shoulders and a muscular build. The thug had boxed in college and he now used that skill to try and take the Cowl down.

The Cowl had to go on the defensive for a few seconds, doing his best to block the blows, but Jerry was coming at him hard and fast, and he wasn't able to counterattack. A few punches even got past his defenses, one blow to his head making his ears ring, even though the punch had been lessened thanks to the mask the Cowl wore. Jerry laughed as the Cowl stumbled backwards, shaking his head to clear it.

But Jerry made a tragic mistake by letting the Cowl back away and not pursuing him. The dark crusader was now able to gather his wits, and in a heartbeat he engaged Jerry again, only this time he was on the offensive.

The smile from Jerry's face vanished, to be replaced by a bloody lip, to then be followed by a powerful blow to the side of the head; a flurry of even more punches soon had Jerry reeling.

Jerry tried to rally himself, and he blocked a few punches and tried to go on the attack again, but the Cowl blocked the blows easily, then he dropped to the ground and swung one leg out in a sweeping motion that knocked Jerry off his feet to fall hard onto his back.

Before Jerry could recover, the Cowl was on him, grabbing Jerry by the head with both hands and smashing him to the ground. Once, twice, and by the third time Jerry was out cold, a small pool of blood seeping out of a jagged head wound on the back of his skull.

"Shit, you killed my boys!" Lenny cried out and shot at the Cowl. The bullet hit the Cowl in the right side, but the Kevlar deflected it. Still, the impact hurt like hell and the Cowl rolled to the side, wincing from the pain. As he came up on his knees, he held a Cowlarang in his hand, ready to throw it at Lenny and end the battle once and for all. But at the last instant he paused, seeing that Lenny was smarter than the other two thugs.

"One more move and the old bitch dies," Lenny snarled, pulling the old woman to him and placing the gun he held at her throat.

"Not if I have anything to say about it," the Cowl said, his voice more of a whisper than a hiss.

"Who the hell do you think you are anyway?" Lenny asked.

"The Cowl."

"The Cowl? Sounds like a bad comic book character," Lenny said with a sneer. "And what's with the getup? You going to a Halloween party? You look ridiculous."

"I think your two friends would disagree, that is if they were still conscious."

"So they're not dead?"

"Not if they get medical attention fast. You can make that happen. Just drop the gun and we can call for an ambulance for your friends."

"Oh sure, and you take me into custody for the cops. Not likely. Those guys are my friends but I'm not gonna go to jail for them. I've already got two strikes against me. I get caught again and I'm going away for life."

"It's better than being dead," the Cowl said, his eyes studying the man, trying to see if there was a chance he could knock the gun from the thug's hand. He took a step forward.

Lenny pushed the gun tighter to the woman's temple. "I said don't move!"

The Cowl stopped, knowing that if he didn't obey, the thug would kill the old woman. The man was scared, and though perhaps not a killer at heart, desperate men did desperate things when forced into a corner. A few feet away, the old woman's husband only stared, his face filled with concern and fear for his wife.

What the Cowl needed was a distraction, and the moment he thought about it, an idea came to him. Slowly, so as not to call attention to the movement, the Cowl slid his left hand to his utility belt. His eyes were locked with the thug's, and he even gave the man a smile, as if he wasn't going to do a thing, that the man was in control of the situation and the Cowl knew it.

His left hand found what he was searching for immediately, as he knew exactly where everything was on his belt by heart. Pressing a small button attached to a transmitter, the engine on his motorcycle suddenly tried to start, as it lay on its side in the center of the alley, left there after the Cowl had jumped off it. But the bike had been in gear when the Cowl had jumped off it to avoid being shot, so though the engine turned over, the motor wouldn't engage. Still, being in gear, the bike jerked about each time the starter was engaged, seeming to Lenny that someone was near it and trying to pick it up and get it running.

Panicking, Lenny shifted the gun away from his hostage's temple, and aimed the gun at the area around the motorcycle, firing twice in quick succession. The second he did this the Cowl went into action. Still holding the Cowlarang, he threw it as hard as he could at the thug's gun arm.

Crying out in pain, the 'rang sank an inch into Lenny's arm, and he dropped the gun, his hand spasming. Then the Cowl was there, sending a punch past the old woman's head and right into Lenny's face, the blow pulping his nose and breaking his left cheek bone.

A muffled scream filled the alley as the thug's nose shattered, and Lenny shoved the old woman away from him, his goal now to escape the Cowl, but the dark crusader wasn't going to let him off that easy.

As Lenny went to run, the Cowl grabbed the man by his jacket and threw him face-first at the alley wall. There was a meaty thunk when Lenny's face struck the wall, the flesh and bone of his face no match for the cold, hard brickwork.

Lenny seemed to stick to the wall for a few brief seconds, then he slowly slid down it, leaving behind a trail of blood and scraped flesh. As he slumped to the ground on his knees, still facing the wall, the once rather handsome face was now nothing but a mangled mass of bloody flesh and muscle. Even if Lenny had countless plastic surgery operations in the future, he would never recover from the wounds he received from the Cowl.

Lenny was still moving, so the Cowl darted in and used the side of his hand like an axe and sent a hard karate chop to the back of the thug's neck. Lenny slid the rest of the way to the ground and remained still, only the twitching fingers on his right hand showing that he was still alive.

Satisfied that his final foe was down, the Cowl turned and went to the old couple, who were huddling together against the wall of the alley.

"You're safe now. Take your wife and go home," he said to the old man, his voice low, more of a growl than anything else. He was angry that these two people had made themselves victims. Yes, there were times when a person was simply in the wrong place at the wrong time, but these two had been beyond foolish by going out on the town with such jewelry and finery. They were like a magnet to the lowlifes that prowled the city each night.

"How can we ever repay you?" the old man asked.

"Well, for starters, don't be so stupid next time you go out. Don't flaunt your wealth. There are people who will always be jealous and won't have a problem taking what's not theirs, even if it means killing to do so. Yes, you have the right to wear what you want and go where you like, but only a fool doesn't understand the inherent dangers of this city."

"I…yes, I see. I…we…were foolish. We didn't think. The city isn't what it once was years go. I grew up in this city, you know. It wasn't always like this." The old man gestured to the fallen thugs. "It used to be a safe place."

The Cowl grunted in response. "Times change, sir. People change, too. The city you knew is long gone, which is why I'm needed now."

"Yes, and I'm glad you showed up when you did. Thank you again, without your help…" The old man sighed, hugging his wife closer. "I don't even what to think about it."

"Go now," the Cowl said, taking a step away and gesturing to the mouth of the alley

Nodding, the old man ushered his wife along, the couple giving the fallen thugs a wide berth. They hurried out of the alley and hailed a cab; they were gone a minute later.

The Cowl watched them go and then went to his motorcycle, which was still lying on its side, the headlight on, the engine silent. He picked it up and started it, the engine rumbling to life despite the fact it had been lying on its side.

One of the thugs groaned softly and the Cowl glanced at the three men. He pulled a small cell phone from one of the pouches on his utility belt and made a quick call to the police, informing them of the three thugs in the alley. "And send paramedics, too. They're not looking too good." The operator on the other end of the line tried to get more information from him but the Cowl hung up on her questions. The phone was untraceable so the report would stay anonymous.

With the rear tire spinning, the Cowl spun the motorcycle around and drove out of the alley, shooting into the street and driving off into the night. He had research to do on the burned building. His night was far from over.

For the rest of the night and into the next morning, the Cowl worked in his lair, searching through file after computer file, and anything else that might give him a clue as to the arsonist's next target.

Finally, he narrowed it down to a list of ten possible buildings, but despite this, it was still as much an educated guess as actual targets, despite the science that had gone into the algorithm he'd written to figure out each one.

Satisfied that he'd done as much as he could do, he finally went to sleep, knowing that the coming night would be the beginning of what would probably be a long stakeout.

The Cowl sat in his car, a painted black and armored vehicle with weapons, and activated by voice commands when needed. On his knees was a laptop, the screen split up into six quadrants, each one showing a different building. The screen changed every three seconds to another screen with the same setup, only now he was looking at more buildings, and when the screen changed yet again, he looked on the same buildings, only now he was seeing their rear entrances. The screen kept changing, twenty pictures in all, showing the front and back of each building.

This was the only way he could stakeout all ten buildings at the same time. He was parked in the exact center of their locations, and it would take less than a minute to reach each one—at least it would, given the way he drove.

Of course, he wouldn't need to drive far, as once he was a block away, he could leave the car and use a grappling line and take to the rooftops. In a city with traffic jams at all hours of the day and night, the rooftops were an excellent means of transportation.

He had been in his car for hours, watching the screen. Now, it was going on three a.m. and though the city never truly slept, it did take a nap from time to time, especially in the wee hours and in particular parts of the city.

Fighting back a yawn, the Cowl took a sip from a thermos, the once hot coffee now lukewarm. Wincing, he swallowed the foul brew, and shifted position in his seat to get more comfortable.

The only issue he was concerned about was using the bathroom, something someone in his profession rarely discussed. Though he was a larger than life person, and prowled the nights of the city as a superhero, he still needed to use the john like any other human being, and getting in and out of his battle suit wasn't something he liked doing. But he'd trained his body for years and could go far longer than a normal human being before he had to use the facilities, and he made sure to drink and eat sparingly when on stakeouts and on patrols.

Still, if his stakeout didn't bear fruit soon, even his iron construction would have had enough and he would need to find a bathroom. Another option was to wear Depends under his suit, but he could never see himself doing that. There was just something so wrong about battling crime in an adult diaper.

Movement on one of the flashing screens caught his attention, and he stopped the rotating pictures and went back to the one where he'd spotted something.

Replaying the picture, he saw a dark figure zoom across the sky on what appeared to be a zip line, to then land on the roof. Who or what it was couldn't be made out given the resolution of the camera, but it was the best lead so far, and he was going to follow up on it.

The building was only two blocks away, so the Cowl left the car where it was parked, slid open the canopy over what was basically a cockpit, and shot a rappel line to the roof of the closest building. An instant later he was being pulled into the night as the cockpit canopy retracted below him.

"Armor," he said into a mic built into his mask. On the ground, the car sprouted metal shields that completely wrapped it from bumper to bumper, encasing the vehicle and protecting it from theft or vandalism.

Then he was on the roof and dashing across it, to then leap off the edge to come down on the next one, which was a few feet shorter, then on to the next roof and so on, until a minute later he was arriving at the building where he'd spotted the dark figure.

Going to the 'roof' access' door, he found it slightly ajar, the lock having been burned off. On closer inspection it looked as if someone had used a blowtorch, the area around the doorknob scorched and blackened, both nothing but molten metal, and still red hot from the heat applied only moments ago. So he was on the right trail, the Cowl thought, as he used the tip of a boot to force the door open. Then he slipped inside the stairwell.

Puling a 'rang, he began descending the stairs. The building had more than thirty floors, and there was no way of knowing where the dark figure he'd seen had gone. All he could do was work his way down the stairwell and see if something caught his eye as to where the culprit might be.

When he was seven floors down, he detected the odor of burning paint coming from below, and he sped up his downward descent. Coming upon the twentieth floor, he found the fire door leading from the stairwell and into the office building in the same state as the roof access door, the lock and doorknob nothing but melting metal.

The intruder couldn't have been leaving a better trail to follow than if he was leaving painted arrows on the wall that pointed to his direction. Of course, assuming it was a *him* was presumptuous. Still, the Cowl bet that when he reached the villain, the odds were that it would be a *he* and not a *she*.

Using the tip of the Cowlarang to open the fire door, he entered the main building.

He had barely cleared the doorway when a blast of fire suddenly erupted before him, enveloping him in a fireball and sucking the oxygen from his lungs.

Though his body wanted to gasp for air, only the Cowl's iron will managed to control his lungs from doing just that, for to do so would kill him instantly as he sucked in the super-heated air, burning his lungs and searing his throat.

Instead, he held his breath and turned away from the flames, his cape taking the brunt of the blast. Still, the heat was unbearable, and the Cowl began running down the hallway, away from the searing heat.

There was the sound of laughter from behind him as the flames followed in his heels. It was just as the heat seemed too much to take that the Cowl reached a junction in the corridor where it doglegged to the left, and he darted to the side at the exact moment a massive blast of fire would have reached him, and this time there would have been no escape.

But he'd made it in time, and the searing flames zipped past him as he fell to the floor, and the wall at the end of the hallway was hit full force by the inferno. Instantly the plaster and paint began to burn, peeling and crackling as it was consumed by the intense fire.

The Cowl had to roll on the floor a few times to make sure there was nothing on him burning, and when he was satisfied, he got to his knees, then his feet, before moving to the corner of the hallway. He needed to see what was waiting for him. Pulling a small mirror no more than an inch in diameter from his utility belt, he used it to peer around the corner.

Coming down the corridor was a man of average height. He wore a bright orange and red costume. His right arm was raised and pointing down the hallway, his left arm hanging by his side. There was a hose running from his back to each arm, where the hose ended at the wrist. Here, the hose connected to a nozzle, a tiny flame flickering like a candle at the end of each one.

The man wore some kind of flamethrower contraption. His upper face was covered with goggles, a small oxygen mask over his nose. On his back he carried two large tanks that could be seen over each shoulder—the fuel for the flamethrower.

The right hand shot out with a blast of fire, forcing the Cowl to seek cover around the corner. The Cowl's battle suit was still smoking from where it had been burned, and even through the fireproof material he could feel the heat from the opposite wall as it burned. The fire sprinklers in the ceiling suddenly came on, dousing the hallway in water, but the heat was so strong that the water did little to nothing to douse the flames. The Cowl detected the odor of napalm, which explained why the flames wouldn't go out on the wall. So his attacker was now using napalm, and for whatever reason the attacker hadn't used it on him upon first stepping out of the stairwell. Thinking back to the two tanks on the villain's back, one must hold standard fuel, while the other held napalm.

The Cowl had been lucky that he'd been hit with a standard blast upon exiting the stairwell, or else he would have been covered from head to toe with napalm, and then even his battle suit wouldn't have saved him.

The fire stream suddenly ceased, and with the exception of the crackling flames and the water raining down, the hallway was relatively quiet.

"Come on out, Cowl. If you don't resist I promise to make it quick and painless. No one can say that Firebug won't show mercy to a defeated enemy."

So now the Cowl had a name to who this arsonist was. Pulling a Cowlarang, the Cowl jumped into the corridor and threw it at Firebug, then he darted back around the corner for cover. He didn't see what came next but he heard the nozzle of the flame-thrower shoot a wide stream of fire, which caught the 'rang and incinerated it long before it reached its intended target.

Laughing, Firebug said, "Oh come on, now, you can do better that that. It didn't even come close."

The Cowl didn't reply, but instead pulled another 'rang and repeated the action. The 'rang flew right at Firebug's head, but at the last instant the villain sent a blast of superheated fire, inciner-ating the 'rang while it hung in the air.

Firebug laughed harder. "Wow, I didn't think it would be so easy to take down the famous Cowl, but it seems your reputation has been highly exaggerated." As he walked, he sent quick bursts of fire before him, which kept the Cowl from attacking.

Looking behind him, the Cowl saw that the corridor he was in ended in a dead end with one door there. Where it led was any-one's guess. But to retreat would mean that Firebug would be free to burn the building to the ground, and the Cowl couldn't let that happen. That was when he realized that though the fire suppres-sion system was working, there were no alarms sounding. That meant Firebug had cut the alarm to the local fire stations, so until the fire was seen from outside the building, there would be no help coming to put out the blaze.

Firebug was at the corner now, and with a blast of flames lead-ing the way, he began to round the corner, expecting to roast the Cowl alive.

But the Cowl had been working on a way to stop the arsonist, and it came in the form of a fire extinguisher mounted to the wall. Just as Firebug stepped around the corner, the Cowl—having taken the red canister off the wall—threw it at Firebug as hard as he could. Then, with the extinguisher flying through the air, the Cowl pulled a 'rang and threw the weapon at the spinning con-tainer.

The razor-sharp tip of the 'rang struck the extinguisher a little from dead center, the puncture releasing the pressurized powder within. Add the intense heat from the blast of fire Firebug sent at the oncoming object, and it was clear to see why the bright red tank exploded, sending out a large white cloud that pushed back the flames.

For a few brief seconds, Firebug was blinded by the white cloud, even as he turned up the heat to burn the white powder from the air. The Cowl attacked, charging at Firebug and sending a high kick directly at the man's chest, which sent the villain flying backwards to fall flat on his back, the twin tanks hitting the carpeted floor with a dull *thunk*.

The Cowl landed on his feet, his fists held up before him, and as he took a step towards Firebug, the arsonist leveled his arms and fired both nozzles so that the flames shot out across the floor.

The Cowl jumped up and to the side, pushing off the wall to stay elevated for a few seconds more, but as he came down he saw that Firebug hadn't shot the blasts to scorch him, but had used his flamethrower like a jet back.

The burst of flames sent him sliding across the floor, and when he reached the end of the hallway, he rolled onto his stomach, got to his knees, and took off deeper into the building.

"Clever," the Cowl said under his breath, then he too, began to chase after his foe.

While Firebug ran away, he continued shooting out flames in all directions. Though this made his trail easy to follow, it also made it difficult, as the napalm burned through plaster and ceiling tiles, to quickly get into the ductwork, where it then continued to spread throughout the building.

Following the burning trail, the Cowl ended up on a floor three below the one where he'd first encountered Firebug. As he rushed into a main section where the room had been split up into cubicles, the ceiling high, the Cowl almost ran right into another fire blast from Firebug.

Ducking to the side and rolling to hide behind a desk, firebug laughed as he bathed the area in red-hot flames.

"You can't stop me, Cowl, sooner or later I'm gonna getcha."

"We'll see about that," Cowl replied, then jumped up and threw a Cowlarang. The weapon zipped through the air as fast as a bullet, hitting Firebug in the chest, but instead of impaling the man, the 'rang bounced off.

The Cowl frowned. Firebug was wearing some kind of armor, perhaps something similar to the Kevlar woven into the Cowl's own battle suit.

"See? What did I just say?" Firebug laughed, having a grand old time. "Besides, who appointed you a servant of the city? What gives you the right to even try and stop me? In the end, you're just another crazy in a costume." Firebug raised both arms, lining up the desk the Cowl was hiding behind. "Just like me!" He fired both nozzles, the desk instantly becoming enveloped in an inferno of flames. The fire was so hot it took only seconds to burn the wooden desk to ash. Firebug walked over to the blackened remains of the desk, expecting to see the charred corpse of the Cowl there as well, but when he moved closer, his eyes went wide to see that the space the Cowl had been occupying was now empty. "What the…" he began to say, and then detected movement above him. Looking up, the Cowl glared down at Firebug from where he'd shot a rappel line to the ceiling, escaping the flames a split-second before they struck the desk.

"Not bad, Cowl, but not good enough." Firebug raised an arm to shoot the Cowl, but the dark crusader dropped down from the ceiling, his cape spreading out to block out the light from the fluorescents in the ceiling still working. Though the cape was singed, it was still more than serviceable for this action.

The room was full of choking smoke as the fire raged around the two battling men, surging within the walls and through the offices one at a time, the roiling flames consuming everything.

The Cowl had put on his oxygen mask, or else he risked becoming overwhelmed by the cloying smoke.

Firebug was about to send a spray of fire at the Cowl, when the dark crusader used another 'rang, holding it like a knife. Before Firebug could get off the shot, the Cowl slashed at Firebug's arm, severing the hose that connected to the nozzle. Immediately, flammable fluid began to spew out of the fuel line, dousing Firebug in the liquid.

Roaring in anger, Firebug jumped away from the Cowl, wanting to gather himself before attacking again. He ignored the fuel spraying the inside of his arm and torso, the fumes surrounding him in an invisible bubble of death, his need to kill the Cowl overriding any form of self-preservation.

"It's over, Firebug, you're done for. Surrender now and I'll see you get a fair trial." The Cowl took a step towards Firebug, his hand held out in what he hoped was a genuine sign of compassion. They had battled and the Cowl had won, for if Firebug even attempted to use his other nozzle, the result would be instant death.

"Over? No, Cowl, it's not over. And it won't be until you're dead!" He raised his good arm, his finger already wrapping around the trigger to the nozzle to send a burst of fire at the Cowl. Incidentally, this was the hose that contained napalm.

"I wouldn't do that if I were you!" the Cowl yelled, but seeing that Firebug wasn't listening, he turned and began running in the opposite direction. "Fine, have it your way."

"Die, you bastard, die!" Firebug screamed, then squeezed the trigger on the nozzle. But the instant the napalm shot out, thrusting forward to chase after the Cowl's fleeing form, the fuel-saturated air around Firebug was also ignited, to erupt in a glowing fireball that completely enveloped the arsonist.

Next, the twin tanks on Firebug's back ruptured as the flames burned the seals around them, releasing even more jets of flammable gas and napalm into the air and consuming the man utterly.

Firebug was lost in an ever expanding circle of flame that roasted the costumed villain alive.

The Cowl knew he was still too close to the growing fireball, and he began running even faster, but though quick, he still wasn't fast enough. The blast was beginning to dissipate by the time it reached the Cowl's fluttering cape, but was still more than hot enough to catch fire to the tail end of the material.

Seeing he was on fire, the Cowl dropped and rolled, trying to put out the flames. But it wouldn't work, the cape covered in burning napalm that would soon spread to the rest of his battle suit. Acting fast, he ripped the cape from his body and threw it to the floor.

Coming to his knees, he looked back at the shrinking fireball.

Firebug was slumping to the floor, where he landed in a heap of scorched flesh. On half his body the costume had been burned off him, and on the other half the material had melded with his flesh. All around Firebug fires raged, thanks to the fuel from the exploding tanks.

In seconds, the entire place would be nothing but flames, and anything living would quickly be dead by either smoke inhalation or from the heat itself.

Coming to his feet, and heedless of the flames burning everywhere, the Cowl ran to Firebug and knelt down beside the still form, planning on picking up the body and carrying it out of the building.

Though Firebug was a criminal, the Cowl wouldn't let the man's body burn in the fire that he'd created if there was a choice. He expected the man to be dead, and he couldn't help but illicit a gasp of horror and amazement to see that Firebug was still alive, if barely. His goggles and oxygen mask had melted around his eyes and nose to become one with his flesh, but the two orbs were still there, flicking back and forth.

"I…I can't see," Firebug whispered, his lips gone, the words barely intelligible. "You…you knew that would happen."

"Yes. I did."

"You could have tried to stop me, but you didn't."

"I know."

"Then why?" Firebug gasped.

"Because it was the only way to stop you."

"By killing me?"

"Yes, if that was the only way then so be it."

There was a dry cracking sound and it took the Cowl a moment to understand that Firebug was laughing.

"But I thought you didn't kill?"

"There was a time when I swore I would never take a life, but….things have changed since I took that oath."

Firebug coughed hard, spitting blood. "Clownface said you were a killer."

The Cowl's eyes went wide at the mention of his arch nemesis. "What did you say? What do you know about Clownface?" He grabbed Firebug and began to shake the man, heedless of the arsonist's injuries. "Damn it, man, tell me what you know about Clownface?"

Firebug managed another cackle. "Screw you," he said, then his chest heaved once and he died, the eyes still open but seeing nothing.

"No, don't die on me, not yet. Tell me what you know!" the Cowl yelled. He gazed down at the charred corpse lying before him, wanting to shake the body some more, make the man talk, even from beyond the grave, but he knew it was hopeless. Firebug was dead; he was beyond talking to anyone ever again. Whatever information he had, it would remain with him in death.

Standing, the Cowl turned and limped away, making for the roof, where he would then return to his waiting car. He had stopped Firebug, there would be no more fires set in the city, but once more he had seen a life taken from the Earth when perhaps he could have saved it.

What was he turning into? Was he so desperate to prevent evil that in turn he was becoming that which he fought each night? And if so, would there come a time when his soul would become so corrupted that he would turn into the very thing he loathed above all else, namely that of a criminal who would take human life without care?

And what would happen then? Would someone else then come after him, thinking that he was the very evil he once tried to keep in check?

These questions and many others were something the Cowl would need to address in the coming future, but for now there was only the need to escape the burning building before he too was consumed in the growing conflagration.

With the fire closing in behind him, it quickly consumed the body of Firebug, a fitting funeral pyre for a man who was an arsonist.

In the distance but coming closer, the sounds of sirens flooded the night.

IN THE CLUTCHES OF CLOWNFACE

It had been two months since the Cowl's battle with Firebug. Sitting perched on top of a building across from the largest bank in the city, he watched as the chaos below continued to become larger.

The standoff had been going on for hours, and now night cast its dark blanket over the city.

There was a perimeter cordoning off the street, and more than two dozen police cars filled the street from end to end, another half at the back of the bank, guarding the exits.

SWAT troopers were everywhere, all lined up with their guns aimed at the front of the bank, while snipers lined the rooftops.

The Cowl sat only twenty feet from the closest sniper, the trooper having no idea he was there, thanks to the shadows and the moonless night.

"Come out with your hands up, Clownface! There's nowhere to run to; the building's surrounded!" the captain said from the center of the police blockade, the bullhorn amplifying his voice so that the entire street could hear him. "You have five minutes to surrender the hostages or we're coming in!"

From within the bank, Clownface's voice came out loud and strong, thanks to his own bullhorn. "You come in here and I'll kill the hostages! I have over thirty people to use as target practice, and I have no problem killing as many as it takes to ensure my freedom! Let me go free, take as much money as I want, and I'll think about not killing everyone as I leave!"

"You know that won't happen, Clownface, I can't allow you to simply go free. But if you surrender, I promise you won't be harmed and that you'll be treated fairly."

Amplified laughter floated out of the bank. "Yeah, sure, and I'm the new Pope. My coronation is next Sunday. No deal, pig. Now, I have a deadline for you, copper! Give me what I want or in two minutes I'm gonna kill the first hostage! Tick, tick, tick; time's a wastin'!" There was a click, the sound of the bullhorn being turned off, which also told the captain Clownface was done talking.

"Okay, men, you heard him," the captain said to the surrounding policeman and SWAT troopers. "We have two minutes or he starts killing hostages. We have to go in."

"But, Captain, if we go in there in an assault, there's no way to know for sure if we can save all the hostages," another officer said.

"Don't you think I know that, Michaels?" the captain replied. "The odds are that people will die in a frontal assault, but at least this way we can save some of them. That madman will kill everyone in that bank to get his way." He turned to the SWAT commander beside him and added, "Sergeant, get your men ready for a full assault. Flashbangs, tear gas, everything you got, use it. That man in there is a stone cold killer. He has dozens of warrants for suspected murders, robbery and assault, and who knows how many other crimes he's done that we don't even know about."

"We'll be ready," the SWAT commander said, then he moved off while talking into his two-way radio to gather his men.

The captain sighed and wiped the sweat from his brow.

"This could make your career if it all goes well, Captain," another cop said from his side.

The captain only grunted. "Maybe, but if it goes the way I think it will, it'll probably ruin it instead." He patted the cop on the shoulder. "Either way, I'm getting too old for this shit. My wife wants me to retire anyway. I probably should, but damn it, I'm just too stubborn to go down without being forced to."

Suddenly from above small objects rained down all around the street before the bank and among the policeman. As the objects struck the pavement, they broke open, releasing a thick cloud of gas that filled the street from end to end in one massive cloud that made visibility almost nil. There wasn't much of a breeze, which only helped the smoke cloud to settle amongst the police. It did its job well, which was to block the bank from the policemen's line of sight.

"What the hell?" the captain screamed. "That damn clown must have some kind of booby traps set up. He must have known we were going into the bank! Damn it, where is everyone?" He tripped over someone's legs. Falling to the asphalt, he managed to catch himself before his face hit the pavement, and he rolled to the side as people ran past him, threatening to step on him. Men and women officers were calling out as they moved amongst the smoke, trying to get their bearings.

The captain, still lying on the ground next to a squad car to prevent getting crushed by feet, was looking straight up at the night sky, or what he could see through the roiling gray smoke.

It was as he was peering upwards that he could have sworn he saw something zip across the sky from a nearby rooftop towards the bank, but the figure was only there for an instant, then it was gone, lost within the smoke. Figuring he was mistaken, and that his eyes were playing tricks on him given the circumstances, he stood up and began trying to gather his people, while the smoke clung to him like thick fog having just rolled in off the sea.

Dropping the smoke pellets everywhere in the street, the Cowl used the distraction to shoot a rappel line from his rooftop to the roof of the bank, then slid across the open expanse between the two buildings. His cape billowed out behind him as he soared through the air, and when he glanced down, he saw complete chaos through the smoke.

He was pleased. The smoke would keep the authorities busy while he entered the bank and saved the hostages, and by doing so make sure no one died.

Reaching the bank, he let go of the rope, and stealthily dropped onto the roof, rolling once to absorb his momentum before coming to a stop on one bended knee, his body crouched low to use as much of the night as possible to remain hidden. He didn't know if Clownface had guards posted on the flat roof. In his hand he held a Cowlarang, the steel tip reflecting the lights from the squad cars below, despite the smoke cloud diffusing the illumination.

It was as he was about to get up and make his way to the roof access door that he suddenly felt a powerful blow to his back, which sent him sprawling forward. Blinded by the pain, he forced himself to roll across the roof, just as another bullet struck the roof in the exact spot he'd been occupying.

He didn't stop rolling until he reached a large air conditioning unit, and only then did he get to his knees and crouch behind the unit. He shook his head to clear it of the flickering lights flashing before his vision, and fought to control his breathing, which came in ragged gasps.

If he had to guess, it felt like he'd cracked a rib from the impact of the bullet that hit him. The lenses over his eyes on his mask had a setting for infra red, and he used it now, scanning the rooftops across the street. There, it was the sniper he'd been close to when watching the bank only moments ago. The trooper had seen movement on the bank roof and had taken a shot, the chaos happening on the street not fazing him in the least.

Feeling around to his back, the Cowl could feel a slight indentation where the bullet had struck him, and only his Kevlar-lined battle suit had saved him from a killing shot. Setting his jaw, he nodded at the SWAT sniper. The man had done his job and done it well, and the Cowl held him no malice, still, he would have to rethink his point of attack next time a similar scenario came up. He knew he had as much to fear from the police as the criminals he hunted. A vigilante, the police didn't approve of his methods and would arrest him as easily as arresting a criminal.

Turning, he saw that he could reach the access door and still keep the air conditioning unit between him and the sniper, so he headed off again, keeping low, hoping another sniper didn't pick him up in their scope before he reached the door and safety.

On the street below, the yelling continued as the men and women of the city's police force dealt with the smoke cloud. The Cowl knew the cloud would dissipate soon. He would need to have the hostages saved by then, or else risk the police storming the bank. Clownface was too smart for the police and the Cowl knew the cops underestimated him. Just because the man dressed like a clown had no bearing on his intelligence. Though a psychopath if there ever was one, Clownface was highly devious and intelligent. The Cowl knew nothing was as it seemed with the evil harlequin, and as he picked the lock on the door and entered into the building, he knew he had to be ready for anything.

The Cowl made his way down the stairwell quickly, and soon was at the door leading into the main floor of the bank. From the other side of the door he could hear talking, and once in a while someone let out a brief scream, as if they had been startled. Edging open the door, the Cowl saw he was in a long hallway. No one was in sight so he exited the doorway, was careful to make sure the door made no sound when it closed behind him, then crept down the hallway. On each side of him were offices, all of them now empty.

At the end of the hallway, the commercial-carpeted floor ended and polished marble began, signifying the main area of the bank. Moving to the end of the hallway, the Cowl crouched low and peered out, studying everything he could see. It was a standard looking room, with a long row of windows for tellers, a few waist-high islands in the middle where customers could fill out deposit and withdrawal slips, and in the far corner were some desks, each lined up in a row, where customers would go to apply for loans or other business the tellers could not help with.

At the moment, there was no one behind the windows or at the desk. The main hall of the bank itself was massive, with large marble columns and a cathedral ceiling, plus stone statues of Roman gods scattered here and there. The bank owners wished to display a sense of wealth to their customers, and did a pretty good job of it. The bank in many ways resembled a museum rather than a financial institution.

Employees and customers alike were all prone on the floor, most looking scared out of their lives.

Lying on the floor near the main doors leading to the street, were the three security guards, all dead with bullet wounds to the chest. They had never seen their deaths coming.

The hostages were spread out in a wide circle in the middle of the floor, and in the middle of them, in the exact center of the circle, stood Clownface, his colorful attire and bright blue hair looking very out of place in a building for financial business.

Walking from side to side outside the circle of hostages, were two thugs belonging to Clownface, both brutes carrying automatic weapons. Each man wore colorful shirts and pants, their shoes painted bright red. They wore colorful wigs as well, and their faces were painted white with red circles on their cheeks, and bright red lipstick on their lips. Of course, compared to Clownface they were poor imitations to what a clown should look like. Clownface, on the other hand, was the epitome of a clown, his makeup perfect, his colorful blue and yellow jumpsuit immaculate—not too baggy but not too tight—and his big floppy shoes with bells on the ends were the perfect size for his body, as was the bright blue wig on his head. The white plastic flower on his breast looked brand new as well.

The Cowl decided he needed to take out the two thugs first, then go for Clownface, who also carried a gun. It was like a bazooka but with a much wider barrel, and was painted in circus colors. What the gun used for ammunition to be fired out of its one foot in diameter muzzle was anyone's guess, but knowing Clownface it wouldn't be good for whoever he was shooting at.

The thugs were on high-alert for anything, and not wanting to get shot with automatic weapons, the Cowl needed to wait for the right opportunity to attack. His battle suit might have been bullet proof, but the human body within could only stand so many impacts from the bullets; the Cowl knew he had to bide his time for his chance to attack, but at the same time he needed to act before the SWAT teams outside barged in.

But before he could move, Clownface began doing something with the hostages, so the Cowl waited and watched, hoping this was the opening he was waiting for.

"Come here, you," Clownface said to a woman, a bank teller by her name tag. He grabbed her by her long brown hair and dragged her across the polished marble floor so that she was now in the middle of the hostages, then he put the giant gun right before her face. "I need to make a point here, so that the cops believe what I say to them, and you're gonna be it, honeypie," Clownface said with a snicker.

The Cowl, seeing the woman was about to be killed, prepared to launch himself at the closest thug, knowing he was out of time, but before he could even move, Clownface fired the gun.

But instead of a bullet or a grenade or something that would kill, what popped out of the muzzle of the gun was a red boxing glove. It hit the woman square in the face, sending her flying backwards. She hit her head on the floor and was dazed, but was otherwise unharmed.

The Cowl stopped and waited, seeing that there was no reason to attack yet, as the woman was fine. Tears rolled down her cheeks and she had a broken nose, but nothing life-threatening.

Clownface seemed as surprised as the hostages at what just happened, and he turned the muzzle of the gun on himself, looking right into the barrel. "Hmm, that isn't right, that isn't right at all," he said, his voice echoing inside the large gun barrel. He squeezed the trigger again and again to no effect.

Looking at the hostages, he went and grabbed another one, this time the bank manager. "Let's try this again, shall we?"

Though afraid, the bank manager managed to keep his composure, assuming that the worst that would happen was that he was going to get hit in the face with a boxing glove. Unlike the woman, he knew he could take a punch and so remained stoic, despite the mad clown aiming a large gun at him.

Clownface leveled the gun at the bank manager's face, the man closing his eyes as he waited to be punched in the nose with the glove, only this time, before Clownface squeezed the trigger, his thumb flicked a switch near the trigger guard. The bank was silent as he squeezed the trigger, the hostages watching quietly, expecting to see another glove pop out. But instead of the same thing happening again, there was a loud pop!, and a moment later, the bank manager had no head, the large bullet then continuing onward to become embedded in the marble floor.

As the headless body slumped to the floor, blood spurting out of the jagged neck opening, brains and bone matter spraying the area six feet in all directions, pandemonium reigned within the bank as the hostages began to scream, and a few tried to run away, making a beeline for the front door. The two thugs quickly stopped their escape with a few well-placed bullets into the floor before them

"Everyone shut the hell up!" Clownface yelled loudly, and when he began aiming his gun at the people, they all quickly grew silent, though more than one still whimpered softly. "That's better. How am I supposed to think with all that racket?" He glanced down at the corpse, the blood still squirting from the neck wound, but with each tick of the clock it was slowing. "So sorry about that, old boy," he said with a grin, then added, "Not!" and began to laugh, the two thugs soon joining in. Clownface turned his gaze on the hostages. "What are you all staring at? I made a joke. Laugh, damn it! Clap!"

At first no one laughed, but in a moment a few forced titters filled the air, then more, all phony. Clapping soon followed. But false or not, it seemed to appease the insane clown, and he closed his eyes and tilted his head back, relishing the accolades.

When Clownface opened his eyes once more, he looked down at his jumpsuit and was appalled to see that his white plastic flower had blood spatter on it, as well as the chest of his jumpsuit. His face changing to one of anger, he peered down at the corpse and began to kick it repeatedly. "Look what you did? You got blood on my new suit!" He quickly lost control, kicking the corpse over and over until the place where he was kicking was nothing but a mess of blood and flesh, a few organs popping out. Each time he kicked the body, the bell on his shoe would jingle chillingly. Glancing down at his red floppy shoe, he saw it was now coated in blood and gore. He looked like he was going to explode, but then he closed his eyes and began to breathe. In and out, over and over, and his lips moved as he counted from one to ten.

Slowly, he regained control.

The Cowl watched silently, taking it all in. Seeing Clownface act as he was, it was a peek into the true mind of the man—a mind that was unstable and deadly.

With one final outtake of breath, Clownface looked at the hostages, then he raised the gun and said, "Next!"

Once more the hostages began to scream, knowing someone was about to be chosen to die.

The Cowl realized he was out of time, too.

He'd hesitated after seeing the boxing glove hit the woman, and then again when the bank manager had been picked, assuming the same thing was going to happen. But he'd waited too long and his indecision had cost a man his life. As Clownface went and grabbed a screaming woman by the shirt collar, the Cowl knew it was time for action.

Standing up, 'rang and bolo in each hand, he charged across the marble floor, directly at the two thugs.

Clownface saw the Cowl first, and he called to his two thugs to get their attention. "Wake up, you idiots, the caped fool has finally arrived!"

Both men looked to where Clownface was pointing, and they brought up their automatic weapons and began firing.

The Cowl zigged and zagged as he darted across the floor, bullets missing him by inches. At his feet, bullets were churning up the floor, sending marble chips flying off in all directions.

It would be impossible for a man to avoid countless bullets coming for him, and so too was it for the Cowl. Though he did his best to stay a moving target, eventually a few bullets hit him, only his Kevlar armor protecting him from mortal wounds.

Still, most were glancing blows and he shrugged off the impacts. But then one bullet hit him right where the sniper had shot him on the roof, and that one caused him to stumble from the pain. As he fell over, he threw both his weapons. The 'rang flew true, striking the gun of the thug and taking a finger or two with it as well. Dropping the gun, blood squirting from severed digits, the thug roared in pain and cradled his wounded hand. The bolo flew true as well, to wrap the other thug around the neck, the weighted ends swirling around the man's face until running out of line. The weights struck the thug's head with meaty thunks, dazing him and causing his shooting to falter.

The Cowl had gone to his knees from being shot, but he forced himself up, pushing back the pain in his side by sheer force of will. The second thug with the bolo was still standing, and already recovering from the bolo around his neck. Acting fast, the Cowl moved across the floor, reached the man and sent a blow to his throat that sent the thug flying backwards, gagging and choking, out of the fight for the time being.

A solo clapping sounded from behind the Cowl and he turned to see Clownface clapping cheerily.

"Well, it's about time, killer. I was beginning to think you weren't going to show up to the party."

"So you were expecting me?" the Cowl asked, taking a step towards Clownface, who raised his large gun and shook his head. "Ah-ah, stay there, killer. I bet even your suit can't take a hit from this baby."

"Perhaps, but you have to hit me first," came the reply, as the Cowl pulled another 'rang from his utility belt. "Surrender now and I'll make sure the police treat you fairly—despite your heinous crimes."

Clownface laughed, and almost seemed to have to go to his knees, he found the Cowl so funny. Finally after a full minute, he regained his composure, and while wiping tears from his eyes, said, "Actually, it's I whom was going to have you surrender to me. If you do, I promise not to hurt you. Well, not too much, anyway."

The Cowl's right hand rose up, the 'rang ready to fly right at Clownface. "And what in that insane mind of yours would ever make you think I would surrender myself to you?"

Clownface shrugged, sliding one foot back and forth on the marble tile, as if he was a bashful teen asking a pretty girl out on a date. "Oh, I don't know. Maybe all the people with guns behind you? Oh, and before you think to fight, you should know those guns have armor-piercing bullets in them. One false move and you're Swiss cheese."

The Cowl turned around to see that a little more than half of the hostages had stood up. Their faces weren't filled with fear any more, now they had looks of murder in their eyes. Each of them held a gun, whether a handgun or a small automatic weapon with a folding stock so it remained hidden under their jackets.

The Cowl had no reason not to believe Clownface about the bullets, for if he was wrong, there would be no way to avoid being hit by so many guns aimed at him. Still, he wasn't about to go down without a fight. Plus, the police would be storming the bank at any second. If he could delay Clownface until then, he would have a chance to break free of the trap set for him. He mentally cursed for being such a fool, and falling for yet another of the evil clown's traps.

"So this was all an elaborate trap to catch me," the Cowl said, trying to stall for time.

Luckily, Clownface took the bait, his vanity something he couldn't say no to. If he had a chance to brag he would take it. "Well, killer, I think it's obvious it was. Our game of cat and mouse is at an end. It's time we have our final reckoning, and I promise when it's over, only one of us will walk away." He smiled and added, "Guess who that'll be?"

Glancing to the front of the bank, the Cowl frowned. Still no cops? What were they waiting for?

Seeing the Cowl distracted, Clownface said, "If you're waiting for the cops to bust in you can forget it."

"I don't know what you mean."

"Oh don't you?" Clownface pulled a cell phone out of a pocket and tossed it to the Cowl. "Here, have a look. That phone gets great Wi-fi—4G and everything. I guess that's good. That's what the kid who sold me the phone told me anyway. I can't have him tell you himself as once he told me how much that phone was, well, I had no choice but to kill him." He shrugged. "Served him right, trying to scam me like that. Who the hell is gonna pay two hundred dollars for a cell phone, I ask you?" He waved the gun in the air as he talked. "And people say 'I'm' crazy."

Looking at the phone, the Cowl watched a news broadcast. The camera was on the police blockade outside the bank, and as he watched, a sniper popped up on the roof of the bank and took a few shots at the police, who ducked down behind the squad cars. So that was why they hadn't stormed the building. The police were dealing with a sniper at the moment.

Seeing what he needed to see, the Cowl tossed the phone away. It broke apart when it hit the floor, the pieces sliding off in all directions.

"Hey, I didn't get the warranty for that. Wow, not only are you a killjoy, but you're a jerk, too."

With no help coming, the Cowl knew he needed to act fast before Clownface got bored and had the former hostages shoot him. Staring at the faces of the former hostages, he saw all shapes, sizes and colors. How Clownface had made these people be his pawns was unknown, but what was known was that they sure looked like they had no problem shooting him if given the order to do so.

The 'real' hostages on the floor said nothing, only stared in fear and shock. None of them had any idea what was going on, and only wanted to live to see the next sunrise.

His hands nothing but a blur, the Cowl went into action. Taking multiple smoke pellets from his utility belt, he smashed them at his feet. Instantly he was enveloped in a cloud of smoke.

"Well, don't just stand there, you idiots! Shoot him, don't let him escape!"

Clownface's former hostages did just that, shooting a massive barrage of armor-piercing rounds directly at where they believed the Cowl to be.

But the bullets hit only air, the Cowl already running for the back of the bank. As he ran, bullets zipped around him like angry hornets. One went past his cheek, so close he could feel the air heat up by its passage. Still, no matter how fast he was, or how clever, there was simply no way an object his size could avoid being shot, and when the first bullet struck him in the thigh he stumbled, faltered, then caught himself and continued onward. He didn't get far before another bullet found its mark, hitting him in the shoulder. He grunted from the pain but still kept moving, despite his vision getting blurry. Adrenalin flooded his system, keeping him conscious. So far the bullets hadn't hit anything important, no vital organs, but he knew his luck would soon run out. At his feet, the marble floor was churned into rock chips as bullets tore into it, narrowly missing his boots by inches.

The cloying smoke was thick, filling the bank from end to end. People were shouting, bullets were flying, and in the midst of it all Clownface was jumping up and down like a spoiled child, angry that the Cowl was escaping.

The Cowl would have made it to freedom if not for some bad luck. After being hit the second time, he got spun around, and though he tried to stay focused, his mind got fuzzy from the pain, and he went in the wrong direction. He ended up coming upon the headless corpse of the bank manager, and before he knew what was happening, he tripped over the body and fell to the floor—right at Clownface's feet as bad luck would have it. Unknowingly, the Cowl had run in a circle, ending up right where he'd begun when dropping the smoke pellets.

Not believing his good fortune, Clownface spun his large gun around, and before the Cowl could rise, the evil harlequin slammed the butt of the gun down on the back of the Cowl's head with enough force to shatter stone.

Only the Cowl's mask, which covered the back of his head and lower neck, saved him from a cracked skull; but it still knocked him out.

Clownface walked in a circle around his fallen enemy, while shouting at the top of his lungs, "Cease fire, you morons! I got him, he's down!"

At first no one stopped shooting, but eventually it began to die down, then was sporadic. One man wouldn't stop, and it took Clownface walking over and shooting the man in the back of the head to stop him. The body dropped like lead weight to the floor, a few of the real hostages sliding out of the way, whimpering in terror.

"Idiot," Clownface muttered.

The floor was littered with spent shell casings, Clownface's red floppy shoes kicking them every which way as he walked around the bank once more, then returned to the fallen Cowl.

"There, that's better. It was getting so that I couldn't think, what with all that racket." Clownface gestured to both his thugs, who were now awake again, the one missing fingers having wrapped his hand in a handkerchief which was already stained dark red. His severed fingers were in his pocket. Wincing from the pain, he hoped they could be reattached when this was all over.

"The cops are gonna bust in here any second, with or without my sniper on the roof keeping them ducking for cover," Clownface explained. "Let's make sure they have a warm welcome when they do, boys."

Both thugs nodded and then aimed their guns at the former 'hostages,' and the real ones as well. The two thugs began to shoot everyone, which was such a surprise that not even one bullet was fired back in response.

In seconds all the people who were hostages, whether fake or real, were spread out on the floor in different poses of death. A few were sprawled with their arms reaching to the bank doors, as if they were trying to crawl to the exit as they were gunned down. But most had fallen exactly where they'd been standing or sitting, the abruptness of their deaths more than a shock to them. Blood seeped from mortal gunshot wounds to coat the floor red, a shiny pool of crimson that reflected the overhead lights in the room. The smoke had begun to dissipate as well.

From outside on the street, the faint echo of the sniper's gunshots could be heard, keeping the police trapped behind their squad cars. But Clownface knew now that with the sounds of gunfire that had erupted from within the bank, the cops were sure to want to get inside, despite the sniper holding them back.

It was time to leave the bank now that the prize had been collected.

Gesturing to the fallen Cowl, Clownface pointed to his two thugs, then the Cowl. "Pick him up, boys, we're leaving." As the two men did as they were instructed, Clownface went to a large yellow duffel bag that had been off to the side. Opening it, he withdrew a large bomb. It had clocks everywhere and other items that served no purpose, such as old cell phones and alarm clock radios. It looked like something out of a Dr. Seuss book. The main part of the bomb was bright red and yellow, with splashes of blue thrown in. It looked as if a crayon box had thrown up, and as the two thugs held the Cowl in their arms, Clownface walked over to the center of the bank and placed the bomb on the floor in the center of the bullet-riddled corpses. "There's enough C4 here to take out this entire building. Hell, probably the ones beside it, too." With a loud flourish, he bent over and pressed one of the myriad of buttons on the bomb and immediately it lit up like a Christmas tree. Digital clocks began to count down, while some flashed 12:00 over and over. Cell phones began to ring and buzzers buzzed, while spinning lights spun around, the lights changing colors.

Nodding in approval, Clownface strolled away, heading to the rear of the bank, the two thugs following obediently. When he was as far back as he could go, the evil clown pulled a floor plan of the bank out of a pocket and studied it, then he took out a smaller bomb from his jumpsuit, and after setting the timer for ten seconds, he tossed it around a corner.

The seconds went by agonizingly slow, but when the counter eventually reached zero, a massive explosion filled the corridor, dust and smoke spewing out of the hallway like the channel for a rocket blast. It died down in less than a minute, and with the air still filled with soot and debris, Clownface walked into the destroyed hallway, the two thugs with the Cowl in their arms right behind him.

The explosion had blown the floor to hell, exposing the sewer line beneath the bank. Water spurted from exposed plumbing pipes, and severed electrical wires sparked and flickered side by side with the water pipes—a dangerous combination if there ever was one. Dust filled the air still, sticking to the faces of the thugs, the Cowl and Clownface.

Making his way into the hole, Clownface put his big gun over his shoulder, the strap letting it sway back and forth. When he was on the ground, or what was like ground inside the hole, as there were piles of concrete and debris everywhere, he called up to the thugs to have them hand him the Cowl. "And be careful with him, you two. I don't want him getting hurt any more than he already is." He smiled manically. "That'll be my job later."

Doing as instructed, the thugs handed the Cowl down to him, Clownface taking the still unconscious man over his shoulder in a fireman's carry, as he swung the big gun back around to face forward. "Shit, Cowl, you need to go on a diet; you weigh a ton," he snickered.

Clownface glanced up at the two thugs, who were about to begin climbing down into the hole as well, when Clownface raised his gun and leveled it at them. "Sorry, boys, but you're not needed any more." He squeezed the trigger, sending a giant bullet at the first thug, then swiveling his hips and shooting the second man while the first thug was being blown apart. The bullets were huge, and much like what had happened to the bank manager, a similar thing happened to the two thugs. The bodies were blown apart from the shots to their torsos, blood and guts raining down around the hole, a spatter of red rain even hitting Clownface. As some of the body parts of the two men slid into the hole, Clownface began to laugh. "Well, boys, when I hired you, I did say there wasn't a retirement plan if you worked for me. Because I knew you wouldn't need one!" He turned and began making his way down the sewer line, still laughing.

He'd just reached the perimeter of what he figured the blast zone would be when the bomb he'd planted in the bank went off, the massive explosion taking out support columns, the shockwave so powerful it simply blew out all the walls on the main floor of the bank, which meant that the rest of the building had nowhere to go but down. The ground shaking from the explosion, Clownface stumbled and fell, the Cowl falling as well.

On the roof of the bank, the sniper paid for by Clownface found out the hard way that the evil harlequin was never going to pay him, and instead had left him to die along with the building itself.

Still, the sniper did his best to escape, racing across the rooftop to where the ladder leading down to the next floor would allow him to then climb down the rest of the building. He managed to get more than halfway across the roof before the ground beneath his feet simply gave way, as if a sinkhole had sprouted on the roof. With a yell cursing Clownface to Hell, the sniper was swallowed alive, to quickly be lost in the destruction as the building collapsed, imploding in on itself.

With the sniper dead along with everyone else Clownface had either used or hired for the bank job, there was no one alive who knew that he had captured the Cowl.

It would take months if not a year for police to comb through all wreckage and figure out what had happened, and even then they might never know the truth.

Deep inside the sewer system, Clownface had recovered from his fall, and though the air was filled with smoke and dust, he powered on, the unconscious Cowl still on his back. The Cowl had tried to wake up, but Clownface had been ready for it and had given the dark crusader an injection that sent him back to la-la land.

Huffing and puffing the entire time from the weight he was carrying, the maniacal clown moved ever deeper into the sewer, all the while whistling a merry tune he'd written himself about torture and death.

The Cowl slowly opened his eyes. His mind was groggy; he had no idea where he was. Concentrating, he tried to remember the events leading up to his awakening, but nothing came to him.

Doing his best to focus his eyes, he tried to get up, but found he couldn't.

A noise came from behind him, the sound of clinking. Trying to twist his head around, he discovered he couldn't. Shifting his body, he noticed his legs were free but both hands were hand-cuffed to the gurney he was lying on—he was trapped. His utility belt had been removed and was hanging on the wall across from his feet. When he tried to move he felt a slight tug over the bullet wounds. Tape, his wounds had been dressed and bandaged.

Someone was humming, the clinking melding with it to create one sound. Closing his eyes, again, the Cowl stayed perfectly still. Whoever was with him didn't know he was awake yet. That was a good thing. He could regain his faculties and take in whatever information he could at the same time, then formulate an escape.

With the humming/clinking going on behind him, he let his mind recover, and as each second passed, he slowly recalled what had occurred and the rest could be surmised given his present predicament.

Clownface had managed to capture him, there could be no other explanation.

As if his mind had been read, Clownface said from behind him in a singsong voice, "I know you're awake, killer! Just hang on a minute, I'll be right there. Oh, we're gonna have so much fun. I guarantee it."

Deciding that playing possum wasn't an issue anymore, the Cowl opened his eyes once more and looked around.

Stark white tile walls, exposed lights, everything painted white for that matter, stainless steel tables and sink, and the wheeled gurney he was on. Overhead in the ceiling, fluorescent lights flickered and buzzed.

Clownface stepped into view, holding a scalpel in his right, cotton-gloved hand. "Have you guessed where you are yet? Tell you what, let's make a game of it." He raised the scalpel to the Cowl's face, waving it before the trapped man's eyes. "I'll give you three guesses. But I warn you, if you don't get it in three, you lose." He took the scalpel away. "Aaaaaand go! What's your first guess?"

Figuring given his circumstances he should play along, at least for now, the Cowl said, "A hospital?"

Clownface made the sound of an annoying buzzer, then sliced the Cowl across the upper arm with the scalpel. The blade was razor sharp and it even cut through the Kevlar suit to the flesh beneath. The Cowl winced in pain but held his tongue, not wanting to give the evil clown the satisfaction of seeing him cry out.

"Oh, didn't I mention that part of the game? Yes, well, if you guess wrong I'm gonna cut you somewhere." He laughed. "It gives the game a little tension, doesn't it?" He grinned evilly, touching the blood seeping from the wound and then staring at it dripping off his fingertips. "So red, blood. God how I love it, the coppery smell, the feeling between my fingers."

The Cowl struggled to break free, the handcuffs clinking against the bars on the sides of gurney. The sound pulled Clownface back from his reverie and he stared into the Cowl's eyes. "Okay, killer, guess number two. Where are we?"

The Cowl didn't say the first thing that popped into his head this time, but instead took another look around the room, knowing if he was incorrect, he would be cut.

A full minute passed, then another, until finally Clownface said, "Will you come on and guess already!"

The Cowl stopped looking around the room and locked his gaze with Clownface. "You didn't say I had a time limit before I had to guess."

"Well, you do now. Guess something or get cut!"

The Cowl glanced at his wound, seeing that the blood had slowed, now the cut only seeping blood. "Are we in a morgue?"

Clownface had already been raising the scalpel to take another swipe at his victim, but before he could bring the blade down, he stopped cold, his smile turning into a frown. "Shit, you figured it out. Good for you, killer." Then he slashed the scalpel across the Cowl's inner thigh, where the Kevlar weave wasn't as thick, slicing into it and the skin beneath.

The Cowl's eyes went wide and he cried out, more from surprise than actual pain. The scalpel was so sharp that the initial cuts didn't hurt, it was after, when the air got at the nerve endings.

"What the hell, Clownface! You said if I guessed correctly I wouldn't be cut."

Clownface shrugged. "I was lying. Haven't you figured out that I do that a lot?"

"You bastard," the Cowl hissed, pulling at his cuffs. He had found out that the right handcuff wasn't locked as tight on his wrist as the left. His thumb wouldn't allow him to get free, but still, at least with the looseness there was a chance, even if it was remote. If he had a few moments without being watched, perhaps he could break his thumb and force his hand through the cuff. A painful proposition, one that would be utter agony, but still, it would be better than death by torture.

Clownface threw his head back and laughed, relishing the Cowl's rage. He went over to a table, which held an old tape player, and pressed the 'play' button on the tape deck. Immediately, music with an undertone of static from the aged speakers filled the room, a soothing, melodic tune with trumpets, cellos and violins. Clownface began to dance around the room, waving the bloody scalpel in the air like he was directing a symphony.

He began to sing: "There are so many ways to kill you, most of them unpleasant, but though I want to kill you more than once, I have to settle for just one time, you dunce." He twirled around the gurney, swaying with the music. "I could chop off your head and bury the body, or I could burn you to a cinder, but both ways are far too fast, the latter making you tinder.

"I could flay you alive, and let you suffer, but both those ways would still be naught but a buffer, for the killing must last quite a while.

"For it needs to last, your torture and pain, or else what would I have to gain?"

Suddenly he stopped dancing and singing and went to the tape player, striking it hard and turning off the music. His face, which had been rather happy, now took a turn for the worst, as if dark clouds were swirling behind his eyes. With the clown makeup on, Clownface's visage was positively chilling, and the Cowl felt a tingle go down his spine despite himself.

"Or," Clownface said with a growl, "I could just slice your throat and watch you bleed out, and finally be done with you." He took a step towards the Cowl, the scalpel in his hand gleaming under the flickering fluorescent lights. The Cowl fought to get free, straining at the handcuffs, but in the end he was only human, and though powerful, his body honed to peak perfection, he still wasn't stronger than hardened steel, no matter how much he might wish it to be. Helpless, the Cowl could only watch as Clownface came towards him, preparing to cut his throat.

Suddenly, the door to the room was shattered, the wood pieces flying off in all directions, thanks to the shotgun blast that blew out the locking mechanism and doorknob section. Before the pieces of the door had fully settled on the floor, half a dozen men in pinstripe suits came charging into the morgue, automatic weapons raised and leveled at Clownface.

"What the hell is the meaning of this?" Clownface demanded, his eyes wide, his face puffing out in anger. "I was right in the middle of a killing!"

The six thugs moved to the side slightly, three on a side, to let one more person into the room.

The Cowl, who had said nothing and merely watched, was more than a little surprised to see the man who entered the morgue. Dressed in a tailored suit, he was tall, with powerful muscles. A fedora topped his head, and below it the hair was dark black. But that wasn't what would make anyone who saw him gape in awe.

It was his face.

The skin on the man's face was a patchwork of flesh, the scars like a roadmap where each graft had been done. The skin was an assortment of shades from multiple donors; from dark black of an African American, to the lighter shades of a Sicilian immigrant. Other spots of the skin were pale, as if the donor had never seen the light of day, and in other places the skin had small freckles. A mosaic of skin tones to say the least, the shapes all different, as if the man's face was a cardboard puzzle and not made of human skin.

"Who the hell are you?" Clownface demanded, "And what's with your face? You look like a jigsaw puzzle that's thrown up."

The man shifted the shotgun he was holding, a scowl crossing the dark face. "Maybe that's why they call me Puzzleface. Ever heard of me?"

"Heard of you?" Clownface scoffed. "No, I haven't heard of you. Do you know how many costumed idiots are in this city? With more popping up every day? Shit, I'm gonna start a convention for all of us." He took a step towards the back wall, his foot moving the gurney the Cowl was on close to him as well. The movement was subtle, neither Puzzleface or the six thugs noticing it. "Now, what do you want?"

"Him," Puzzleface said, gesturing to the trapped Cowl, who looked back with his eyes creased. His wounds had mostly stopped bleeding at least, though they stung terribly.

"Him? Well you can't have him, he's mine. I caught him, I get to kill him." Clownface glared at Puzzleface. "How'd you find me anyway?"

"I've had people I paid off keeping an eye out all over the city for you. Homeless, some cops, even a few old ladies. I got people all over the place. I told them to watch for you, and sure enough, a few hours ago I got a tip someone saw you coming into this old building."

Clownface remembered seeing a homeless man in the alley as he'd come up from the sewer and then into the back door of the building the morgue was in, carrying the Cowl on his back still. At the time, he hadn't thought much of it, but now looking back, he'd made a grave mistake.

He'd barely registered the bum as a possible threat, like most people thought, the homeless were invisible to the rest of the city's population.

"Why do you want him so bad anyway?" Clownface asked, moving even closer to the wall, while sliding the gurney with him.

"I have my reasons. But let's just say for the sake of being equable that I owe him for this face and I plan on repaying my debt to him—in blood. His blood." He jabbed a finger at the Cowl who said nothing in reply.

Clownface merely nodded. "Well, maybe that's so, Patchwork, but…"

"That's Puzzleface, damn it," the crime boss interjected.

"Yeah, right, whatever," Clownface said, not caring in the least. "But sorry to tell you this, but this prize is mine to kill. I worked damn hard getting him here and if anyone's gonna kill him it's me." He patted the Cowl's chest. "I deserve it."

Puzzleface sighed, tired of the debate. The Cowl was his and he wasn't about to let some fool clown stop him. Raising his shotgun, he yelled to his thugs, "Kill that damn clown already! But the man who accidentally shoots the Cowl will answer to me with their head on a spike!"

"That's my cue to go," Clownface said, and while Puzzleface was giving the order to fire, the evil clown reached up to the wall where there was a hook. Pulling on the hook, the entire section of wall and part of the floor where he and the Cowl were began to spin around. As the bullets began to fly, the wall had spun so that only a blank wall was hit, Clownface and the Cowl safe on the other side.

Clownface grabbed the gurney and began to push it down the long hallway, only a string of naked bulbs hanging from the ceiling giving off illumination.

"I got that idea from watching Abbot and Costello one day. They were in a haunted house and the werewolf or mummy or whatever pulled that trick."

As Clownface pushed the Cowl down the long hallway, the tiled wall inside the morgue was smashed to pieces from dozens of bullets.

Dust filled the air from the shattered tiles and Puzzleface let out a scream that made every thug stop moving, for fear that their boss would turn his wrath on one of them. Finally, after a full minute of ranting and raving, and shooting the wall a few more times, he calmed down.

Lowering his shotgun, Puzzleface pointed to the first three of his men, then the other three. "Don't just stand there looking like a bunch of morons, get over there and get that wall open!"

"We going after them, Boss?" a thug asked.

"You better believe we are, Rocco. The Cowl's mine, and that clown is gonna suffer." He gripped his shotgun so tight that his knuckles turned white and for a moment it looked like even the metal of the gun would bend. "When I get through with that damn clown, he's gonna wish he'd let me shoot him."

The gurney's wheels rattled over the uneven floor of the disused hallway. It had once been used as a service corridor, but was boarded up long before the rest of the morgue had been finally closed down five years ago due to budget cuts.

Clownface hummed the lyrics to the song he'd sung earlier while the Cowl remained silent.

"Don't you worry, killer. Once I get you to another of my hidey-holes, we'll get right back to me killing you. I promise," Clownface said, patting the Cowl on the chest.

"I can't wait," the Cowl replied through gritted teeth.

Clownface was cheerful at escaping the crime boss, and he was in a chatting mood. "So, who was that guy, killer? He acted like he knew you."

"I've never seen him before today," the Cowl said, though he was wracking his mind for who the crime boss could be. In all his escapades, he'd never come across a man whose face resembled a jigsaw puzzle made of flesh.

"Well, killer, he sure as hell knows who you are." He made a tsking sound. "If I hadn't gotten us out of there, you'd be nothing but a bullet-riddled corpse—or worse."

"Thanks," the Cowl replied sarcastically.

"Oh, don't thank me, thank the men who built the revolving wall. In fact, you actually can. Here they are now." Clownface slowed the gurney as he and the Cowl approached three corpses lying on the floor, the limbs of the bodies strewn in all different directions, as if they had been dumped there after being killed, the bodies like limp and malleable ragdolls.

"Of course, they were kidnapped and forced to do it, then I killed them later so they couldn't talk. Hi ya, boys, what's cookin'?" Clownface waved to the three corpses. Each one had a bullet wound to the head. Clownface shook his head as if in contempt. "Oh, those Union boys, always lying down on the job." Upon seeing Cowl's reaction to the three corpses, Clownface added, "Well, it's cheaper than paying Union wages!" He laughed long and loud.

Light could be seen at the end of the hallway, and the Cowl knew if he was going to do something to escape his fate, he'd better do it now. The entire time he was being pushed down the long tunnel, he'd been working at his handcuffs.

With no other options, he'd managed to break the thumb on his right hand, the pain excruciating; it had been all he could do not to cry out when he'd done it, for fear of alerting Clownface. Now he was waiting for the exact moment to try and pull his hand free of the cuff. Not that it would be as simple as that.

Upon reaching the end of the long hallway, Clownface— humming once more—walked from where he was pushing the gurney, which was by the Cowl's head, and moved past the Cowl until he was at the opposite end of the gurney, his back to the Cowl for a few brief seconds as he opened the door to push the gurney through the doorway.

The Cowl knew it was now or never, so the instant Clownface's back was to him, the Cowl began yanking at the hand with the broken thumb, forcing the wrist through the handcuff.

Gritting his teeth so as not to make a sound, he began sliding his hand through the cuff, but though his thumb was broken, it was still far too tight to just slide through.

But the Cowl wasn't about to give up, for if he didn't do something now, there would be nothing to stop Clownface from killing him.

The black glove on his hand was pushed off as he slowly forced the lower part of his hand through the metal, but something had to give, much like a circular peg going into a square hole, and given that flesh was weaker than steel, their could be only one outcome.

His skin began to tear, to separate from his arm, much like a piece of cooked chicken skin being pulled from a cooked chicken straight from the oven.

Then again, as the Cowl slowly, inexorably pulled his hand free, he was reminded of stretching taffy. The glistening muscles of his arm were quickly exposed to the air, and the second this happened, he was blinded by pain, the feeling indescribable.

He was in his own world, now, one where pain and suffering were his only companions. For those few brief seconds as he attempted to break free, Clownface was gone, as was the long hallway; there was just himself and the pain of his right hand and arm.

On the up side, his bullet wounds, scalpel cuts, cracked ribs, and broken thumb weren't an issue anymore, as more serious wounds now took precedence.

Blood squirted from where his skin was torn from his arm, and it acted as a natural lubricant to help him pull his hand free. Though the entire process took only seconds, to the Cowl it felt like an eternity, one where if he closed his eyes and imagined the severity of the pain, it would seem as if his hand was being burned off with acid.

At the same moment that Clownface began to turn around after opening the door, the Cowl, his jaw taut, his lips pressed so tightly together that they turned blue, yanked one last time, his hand popping free of the handcuff with a squelching sound.

"What the hell! Oh no you don't, not this time!" Clownface yelled, referring to the Cowl's knack for escaping Clownface repeatedly in the past. He ran the few steps between him and the Cowl, while pulling a knife from the waistband of his jumpsuit. He would just kill the Cowl here and be done with it, then he would put the body on display somewhere where the entire city could see it—maybe hang it from a window in City Hall.

Seeing Clownface coming at him with a bared knife, the Cowl ignored the blinding pain in his hand and wrist and went on the attack, despite being still attached to the gurney.

Sliding off it to stand up, he kicked out with a leg, his heavy black combat boot hitting Clownface in the right knee. There was an audible crack as the bone and tendons in the knee shattered, and Clownface began falling head first to the floor.

Out of pure reflex, Clownface spread out his hands before him to stop his face from connecting with the floor, but because of this he didn't have time to think about the knife in his right hand. The tip was pointing back to his chest, and as he fell onto the floor, he inadvertently impaled himself on his own knife.

As he landed on the floor, the blade sliding into his chest, and missing his heart by less than an inch, he let out a soft, "Eek."

But the killer clown only stayed that way for a second, then he rolled onto his side and got to his knees, ignoring his damaged kneecap. The knife handle was jutting out of his chest, only a small patch of blood on his jumpsuit. The blade was staunching the flow of more blood.

"That hurt, you asshole," Clownface whispered, his eyes filled with insanity, so much so that he ignored the blade in his chest. "You'll pay for that." Standing before the Cowl with his weight on his good leg, he reached up and wrapped his right hand around the handle of the knife, and with his gaze locked on the Cowl's face, he slowly pulled it out of his chest.

Blood began to spurt from the wound the instant the knife was removed, seeping into the jumpsuit and spreading across Clownface's torso, but the evil harlequin ignored it. His focus was only on the Cowl.

With a loud scream he lunged at the Cowl, the knife sweeping around in a wide arc to stab the dark crusader. But the Cowl had an arm free, even if the hand was practically useless, and he raised it, blocking the downward sweep of the knife. Roaring in anger, Clownface jumped away, then came in again, slashing at the Cowl's face.

Not fast enough to avoid the attack, the blade sliced a thin furrow in the Cowl's chin, a line of blood seeping from the wound to splash down his chin and then fall to the floor.

Laughing manically at having scored a hit, Clownface renewed his attack. Pushing the gurney with him, the Cowl backed away, wanting to get as much room as he could to fight in the hallway that was only six feet from wall to wall.

He barely did this before Clownface came at him again, hacking and slashing, blood dripping from his mouth as he coughed up red bubbles thanks to his chest wound. The Cowl figured a lung had been punctured.

For a full thirty seconds, Clownface did his best to kill the Cowl, but the mad clown couldn't get past the Cowl's defenses. Running out of patience and feeling himself growing weak from blood loss, Clownface ran at the Cowl, hoping the move would take the Cowl off guard, as he didn't expect Clownface to do something so foolish.

But the Cowl was ready, and as Clownface came at him, the Cowl kicked out again, connecting with the other knee this time.

Once more a loud crack filled the long hallway, and with both knees now shattered, there was no way for Clownface to remain standing, and the man plummeted face first to the floor.

This time he made sure to keep the knife away from his body.

Laughing like a gibbering idiot, Clownface pushed off the floor with his arms, then somehow got to a sitting position. Both his legs were ruined and he couldn't stand. But he did begin to drag himself forward, the knife slapping the floor each time he moved his hands before him to pull his body along.

"I'll never stop, Cowl. Until I see you dead I'll keep on coming. I don't care how many innocents I have to murder to make that happen, but sooner or later I will kill you."

"I believe you," the Cowl said, and he stepped towards Clownface, and when he was close enough, he kicked the knife from the mad clown's hand. It bounced away to slide a few feet, then stopped.

When the Cowl was standing before Clownface, he reached down with his free hand, ignoring the pain, and with only his four fingers, he grabbed Clownface by his jumpsuit and picked him up so they were face to face.

"I guess this is where you take me to jail," Clownface said, spitting blood, which struck the Cowl in the face. "But let's swing by the hospital first, all right? I need to get patched up so I can later make my escape from jail. Then we can do this all over again."

"No, I don't think so," the Cowl growled, and with surprise clearly on Clownface's face, the Cowl spun the mad clown around and positioned him so that the Cowl was able to use his cuffed hand, as well as the free one, to hold the villain's head between them. Clownface was on his knees, now, and if he felt the pain of being in this position, he gave no sign.

"Wait, what are you doing?" Clownface yelled, bloody froth spewing from his mouth.

"Killing you," the Cowl said flatly as he prepared to twist Clownface's neck, thus breaking it.

"But you can't kill me, it goes against your moral code or some such thing. Look, all that shit about calling you 'killer'? It was a joke, I'm a clown. I joke all the time."

The Cowl ignored Clownface, his body beginning to tense as he prepared to twist the villain's neck.

"But…but if you kill me then I win our game. By killing me like this, when I'm clearly helpless, you'll become a true killer.

Besides, you need me, Cowl. Without me, you're just a nut running around in a black costume. You need an arch villain like me to be complete." While he talked, Clownface slid a hand down the left side of his body, until it reached the top of his floppy red shoe. Sliding fingers inside it, he slowly withdrew an ice pick. One could never have enough weapons secreted on his body, was Clownface's opinion.

The Cowl hesitated, the last words from Clownface sinking in, and he realized though the man was totally insane, he made good sense.

If the Cowl killed Clownface in cold blood, then he was no better than the criminals he fought each night throughout the city.

But before the Cowl could say anything, Clownface swung his arm out and around in a wrapping motion, the hand holding the ice pick directed at the Cowl's right thigh.

The ice pick was sharp, and it penetrated the Kevlar weave of the Cowl's battle suit, then sank deep into his leg.

Roaring with pain and anger, the Cowl, still holding Clownface's head in his hands, instinctively did what he'd been planning. He snapped Clownface's neck, a softer crack filling the hallway.

Clownface's head was nearly twisted all the way around, so that though the body faced away from the Cowl, the painted visage was looking right up at him, thanks to the neck now having nothing to support the head, and the head tilted backwards slightly.

It looked as if Clownface had gotten to his knees before the Cowl, had faced away, then the clown had turned his head around and looked up at the standing Cowl, only the body had remained rooted to the floor.

It was a macabre sight to behold, if anyone had been in the hallway to witness it.

Pulling the ice pick out of his leg with a grunt, the Cowl shoved Clownface's body away from him; it toppled to the floor, and this time there would be no rematch. Clownface was down for good; his evil had been ended forever.

"I guess you win, Clownface, I'm a cold-blooded killer now," the Cowl said. "Congratulations. But don't worry about me not having you to fight. I'll get a new arch villain. This city is teeming with criminals in costumes, if you hadn't noticed."

Using the ice pick, the Cowl got to work picking the lock of the handcuff on his other wrist. It was hard going, as he couldn't use his broken thumb, and each time he moved his hand the torn skin sent waves of agony through his body. Still, the pain kept him focused, and in less than a minute he'd unlocked the second handcuff. He'd been taught by some of the best magicians in Las Vegas on how to pick locks, escape from straitjackets, and other useful tools of the trade, so even with a broken thumb, using an ice pick to pick a handcuff lock was child's play for him.

When he was free, he thought about going back for his utility belt, but when a muffled explosion sounded from far down the hallway, and then the sounds of men's voices screaming and yelling floated to him, he knew that wouldn't be an option. Puzzleface hadn't taken his loss of the Cowl in stride and had been hard at work trying to break through the wall to renew the chase.

If an unauthorized person had tried to open the myriad of pockets on his utility belt, the belt would self destruct. No doubt that was the explosion he heard, the resulting explosion also blowing through the wall.

The voices were getting louder now, and a few angry words could be made out, such as, "We lost three guys... Damn belt blew up…" and other words that were soon lost in the jumble of multiple people talking at once and the distortion of the echo.

Gunshots sounded, and a moment later the doorframe behind the Cowl erupted in plaster and dust from the impacts. Thinking fast, the Cowl grabbed the gurney and stood it on end, so that it became a hasty shield. No sooner did he do this than bullets pounded the gurney, the loud sound of metal on metal reverberating throughout the tunnel. With the gurney being struck over and over, bullets whining all around, the Cowl began moving to the doorway at the end of the hall, having to walk backwards so he could keep his shield between him and the coming bullets.

Clownface's body absorbed a number of stray rounds, the body moving slightly as the bullets hit the corpse.

Upon reaching the doorway, the gurney wouldn't fit through the doorframe when it was standing straight up, so the Cowl propped it at the doorway and then stepped through. He found himself in another building, a storage facility by the looks of it. Spotting the EXIT sign on a far wall, he limped to the door. Pushing down on the metal roll bar, an alarm began to sound, but he ignored it, and stepped through the doorway and the freedom beyond.

As the Cowl moved down the alley and into the street, his mind raced with all that had occurred this night. Life changing events had happened, there was no question about it.

On top of the conflicting emotions that filled him about the death of Clownface, there were even more pressing matters to deal with.

A new enemy was gunning for the Cowl.

Who was this Puzzleface? Another criminal, sure, but this one had inadvertently saved him from the certain death of being murdered by Clownface. But the Cowl had no illusions that if Puzzleface had an opportunity, the man would kill him just as easily as Clownface would have.

Still, the Cowl would forever have to accept that if fate hadn't intervened in the guise of Puzzleface arriving to stop Clownface, the mad clown would have killed him this fateful night in the abandoned morgue.

Feeling like a truck had run him down, to then back up and do it a few more times, the Cowl hailed a cab.

The cab driver looked at the Cowl and his black outfit, and the blood practically covering him from head to toe, and assumed that this guy was nuts, but when the Cowl pulled out a hundred dollar bill from a hidden pocket on his battle suit and tossed it to him, the cab driver couldn't have cared less if the Cowl had been stark naked. Money was money and he had three kids to feed, and a wife who liked to go on shopping sprees.

The Cowl was driven to where his armor-plated car was parked, and he ducked into the alley and got into the cockpit.

As the car rumbled to life, he set out on his next destination, driving one-handed, his damaged hand lying in his lap.

He needed to pay a visit to one of the many doctors he had on private payroll to patch him up, then he would return to his lair and sleep for a week, if not longer.

THE REVENGE OF PUZZLEFACE

Bullets zipped by the Cowl's head, threatening to end his vigilante career. Trapped behind a pile of shipping crates, he desperately tried to think of a way to turn the tables on his adversaries.

Across the massive abandoned warehouse, more than a dozen thugs were waiting for their chance to attack, and only the Cowl's 'rangs had kept them at bay. Leading the thugs was a new face who wanted the Cowl dead, a face covered with a patchwork of flesh and scars.

Puzzleface stood behind his men, yelling orders at them, rallying them for the attack that the Cowl knew was coming.

The Cowl looked down at the dried blood coating his black gloves. He couldn't feel how sticky the blood was through the material, but it still felt as if he could. Despite himself, he thought back to how he'd ended up in this tenuous situation.

When Puzzleface had been spotted robbing a high-end jewelry store, the APB going out over the police scanners, the Cowl had been close by, and he'd taken to the rooftops. He'd beaten the police by more than three minutes, throwing a wrench in the crime boss' best laid criminal plans.

"You!" Puzzleface screamed when the Cowl dropped down from a vent duct in the ceiling, taking out three thugs before the men even knew he was upon them. "I've been looking for you ever since you got away from me when Clownface had you. And now after all that time you drop right into my lap." He grinned, the gesture looking more like a scowl. "Someone must like me upstairs." He gazed up at the ceiling, and at God, and whatever deity was hanging around in the heavens bestowing favorites on willing subjects.

It had been more than five weeks since Puzzleface had saved the Cowl from certain death by Clownface. In all that time, the Cowl had been recuperating, and only today had he ventured from his lair to begin fighting crime once more. His ribs still hurt and his gunshot wounds were healed but tender. He'd planned on just going out into the city to see what he could find, such as a mugging or an attempted rape. He knew he wasn't ready for a battle with Puzzleface and his goons, but he also knew deep down that even if he'd known in advance that this meeting was going to happen, he wouldn't have shied away from it.

Clownface was dead, killed by the Cowl's own hands, but no sooner did the news of his death become known throughout the criminal underworld, than more costumed villains came out of hiding, wanting to take the crown of the fallen harlequin for themselves.

"I don't know why you want me so badly, Puzzleface, but I can tell you right now, it's not gonna happen."

"You want us to get him, Boss?" one of the three remaining thugs asked.

"No, Lou, not here," Puzzleface said, then he went around the counter, where the glass cases had all been smashed, and he leaned over and grabbed something that was on the floor.

At the sound of a frightened shriek, the Cowl knew what Puzzleface was doing, and a moment later, the man stood up holding a woman by her hair. She was thin, with a mousy face and hair that looked like she had just gotten out of bed. Tears rolled down her cheeks, adding to the ones that had already dried there. By the nametag on her blouse it was obvious she worked in the store.

"You make one move towards me or my men and I'll kill her," Puzzleface said, taking a knife and placing it on the woman's throat."

"If you so much as harm a hair on her head I'll kill you," the Cowl growled, but he held his ground, not wanting to see the woman harmed. Seeing her trapped in Puzzleface's embrace, a flashback of his time at the bank with Clownface came into his head. Then, he'd witnessed a man get his head shot off by the mad clown.

He made a vow to himself right there in the jewelry store that this woman would live to see the end of the day.

Outside, the sounds of police sirens floated into the store.

The police had arrived.

One of the thugs went to the front door, opened it a little, and began spraying the entire street with bullets from his automatic weapon. The police officers ducked for cover, while windows were smashed and tires were blown out on the squad cars.

"Jesus Christ!" the captain yelled as safety glass from a passenger side window rained down on him as he crouched low on the ground. "They have assault rifles! Someone call SWAT in, we don't have the firepower to deal with this!" He rolled his eyes. "It's the bank job all over again!"

Inside the jewelry store, the thug stepped away from the door, the muzzle of his weapon smoking in the cool air. "That should hold 'em for a while," he grinned.

"Good job, Bruno," Puzzleface said with a scowl. He jabbed the knife at the Cowl accusingly, then placed it on the woman's throat again. "Now drop your weapons and take off that utility belt or the broad gets it." He pressed the tip of the sharp edge against her skin so that a thin bead of blood began to form. "I won't tell you again."

The three remaining thugs moved to surround the Cowl, who bent low, a 'rang in his hand.

"You heard the boss, drop that stuff or else," a thug warned.

"Last chance, Cowl," Puzzleface added, then he pressed the blade even deeper. The woman let out a weak whimper and closed her eyes, terrified she was going to die.

"Hey, miss," the Cowl said and the woman opened her eyes. "I won't let him hurt you. I promise." He looked at Puzzleface, who now wore a wide grin. "Okay, I'll do as you say."

He dropped the Cowlarang in his hand, then went to the clasp for his utility belt, but just before he would have unhooked the clasp, he shifted his hand and pulled out a smoke pellet. In the blink of an eye, he threw the pellet to the floor, the cloud of condensed gas becoming white smoke, blinding the three goons and causing them to cry out in surprise. Having kept Puzzleface's position in his memory as the smoke cloud filled the entire store, the Cowl pushed past the thugs to save the woman.

"You shouldn't make promises you can't keep, Cowl," Puzzleface said just before he dragged the knife across the woman's throat, severing her jugular, her life's blood spewing out of the jagged wound.

"No!" the Cowl screamed, but it was already too late.

Seeing the Cowl break through the cloying smoke and jump over the counter, the crime boss pushed the gagging woman away from him, then turned and ran for the back of the jewelry store. "Come on, boys, it's time to go!"

"But what about the guys Cowl took down?" one of the thugs asked as he followed Puzzleface.

"Leave 'em. If they're stupid enough to get knocked out, they deserve what they get from the cops."

As the Cowl screamed "No!" at seeing the woman cut, he threw something at Puzzleface's retreating back, something small that landed on the crime boss' suit near the collar. It was tiny enough that the man never knew it was there.

With Puzzleface in the lead, he led his thugs outside, where more of his goons had been in a standoff with the police. A van covered in metal plates was waiting by the back door, and when Puzzleface appeared, the sliding door to the van opened, and Puzzleface and his three men jumped inside.

"Get us the hell out of here, Marco!" Puzzleface yelled, the driver doing just that. The other men that had kept the police from approaching also got into the van, and with a screeching of tires, it took off, straight at the police blockade at the end of the parking lot.

Puzzleface stuck his upper body out of the passenger van window and began shooting at the police with an automatic weapon.

Windows shattered and tires exploded, the van dodging to the far left of the blockade, where there was the tiniest of gaps between the farthest squad car and a stone pillar that made up one side of the parking lot entrance.

When the front bumper of the van hit the pillar, stone and debris flew off in all directions, the pillar demolished to nothing but an uneven stump.

The van shuddered from the impact but kept right on going, its right side scraping the closest squad car and rocking the cruiser on its shocks.

Then it was free and squealing down the street, as a hail of bullets followed to no avail.

As the Cowl landed behind the counter, he caught the woman just as Puzzleface shoved her forward. But he didn't drop her and chase after the crime boss. Instead, he gently placed her on the floor, cradling her head in his gloved hands, the back of her neck resting on his knee.

He quickly placed his hands over her spurting neck wound but the blood only squirted through his fingers.

Choking on her own blood, the large gash in her neck pulsing with each beat of her heart, he knew she'd be dead in less than a minute.

"I'm sorry," he whispered, cradling her head and rocking back and forth. "I'm so sorry. I was supposed to save you."

Spitting bloody froth bubbles, the woman tried to say something but only unintelligible gurgles came out. Then her eyes fluttered and she went still.

The Cowl gazed down on her still face for a few moments, then he slid her head to the floor, closed her open eyes with a bloody finger, and stood up. Looking at his black gloved hands, he held them palm up before him, staring at the blood coating them, as if the blood itself was accusing him of the crime of murder.

He squeezed his hands closed, the blood seeping out from the clamped sides, then he ran to the back of the building.

Puzzleface would pay for the callous murder of an innocent; he swore it on his life.

Upon reaching the back of the jewelry store, he dashed through the back rooms until coming to the rear exit.

Bursting through the door, he found the police in disarray, a stone pillar shattered, and Puzzleface gone, having made his escape only moments ago.

One of the police officers spotted the Cowl as he exited the building and a cry of alarm went up. A second later, a hail of bullets was directed at the Cowl, but he darted to the right and ran away. One bullet grazed him but his Kevlar-lined battle suit easily deflected the bullet. Then he was around the building and shooting a zip-line to reach the next building's roof. By the time the police reached his former position, he was gone, now racing across the rooftops.

Three blocks away and safe from prying eyes, he dropped back to the ground, where his motorcycle was waiting. Hidden behind a pile of trash, he pulled the bike free and climbed on. He started the engine, and as it idled softly, he took out a small device the size of a cell phone and turned it on. He waited a few moments for it to boot up, then pressed a few of the small touch-screen buttons on the bottom.

A section of the city was displayed on the screen, and in the center of it, moving down a street, was a blinking dot.

The Cowl grimaced, but it was really a grim smile. The tracking device he'd thrown at Puzzleface as the man left the jewelry store was operating perfectly. It would be a simple matter to track the man to his hideout.

Then the reckoning would begin.

It had been easy to infiltrate the warehouse that Puzzleface called his hideout, and even easier to take down the two thugs on guard duty on the rooftop.

Dropping down via a rappel line, the Cowl had begun searching the warehouse for Puzzleface and his men. He found it rather ironic that Puzzleface was using an old, abandoned warehouse. Thinking back to other villains he'd battled in the past, it seemed like he was always in an old warehouse. Were there no other locations a criminal could make their hideout?

It hadn't taken long to find the crime boss either, and in fact it was Puzzleface's men who had spotted him first, as he crept along the massive aisles, of which crates piled high with unknown items towered over the Cowl as he made his way down each one.

A yell of alarm had gone out as the thug—who had been going for a smoke—unslung his automatic weapon and began shooting at the Cowl, heedless of where the bullets might go.

One bullet zipped through the Cowl's cape, leaving a small hole in the material. But that was the only one that even got close, as the Cowl was on the move at the first shot.

Rounding the end of an aisle, he almost ran right into another thug.

Caught by surprise, the thug looked blankly at the Cowl, but it was only for a split-second, and as the man raised his weapon, the

Cowl sent a punch to the gunman's throat, making the guy drop the gun and fall to his knees, gagging.

More bullets filled the air as two more thugs from further down the aisle began shooting. Running again, the bullets all flew past him, and the Cowl decided it was time to attain higher ground.

Rounding another aisle, he was out of sight of the thugs chasing him, so he jumped onto the framework of the shelving unit that made up the aisle and began climbing.

Just as he reached the top, the thugs converged on his former location, all yelling and talking at once, as each asked the other where the Cowl had gone.

The Cowl began running along the crates stacked on the top shelf, keeping low in case someone looked up.

When he reached the end of the aisle, he jumped across the divide to the next shelving unit, then continued onward.

He was just jumping to the next aisle, wanting to then circle around and take the thugs from behind, when Puzzleface appeared at the end of the aisle, a small LAW rocket propped on his right shoulder. "I'm going to enjoy this," he grinned as he lined up the Cowl in his sights, then pulled the trigger without hesitation. The rocket streaked from its housing tube, a trail of white exhaust smoke blasting out of the back of the tube. Puzzleface tossed the expended, one-use rocket tube to the cement floor of the warehouse, then began running away, knowing what was coming next.

The Cowl landed on the edge of the next aisle, just as the small missile struck the support beam at the end, only ten feet below where the Cowl landed.

The structure began to collapse immediately, as shrapnel and debris, plus what was inside the crates, was strewn out in all directions. Before the Cowl knew it, and as the unstable footing beneath him collapsed, he found himself falling along with the rubble that had once been the shelving unit and its contents.

Puzzleface laughed loudly as he turned to see the shelving unit explode into a thousand pieces of metal and other debris. At last, he was getting his revenge on the Cowl for what had been done to him.

It had been a little over two months since Puzzleface awoke in the hospital, handcuffed to the bed, his face a mangled mess of skin and cracked bone, his nose flattened to the point of nonexistence.

"Doc," he'd said upon waking, the doctor hovering over him. "What the hell happened to me?"

"You were found in an alley with some other men, all with different injuries. Yours were some of the worst, I'm afraid," the doctor said matter-of-factly.

He gazed down at his body. It seemed to look okay to him. Both his arms were there, so were his legs, none of them in casts. "What's wrong with me?"

The doctor looked down at his feet, as if he was hesitating, then he said while holding up a small mirror, "Perhaps it would be easier to just show you. But brace yourself, it's not pretty." But before the doctor handed the mirror to him, the man added, "But before you lose control, I need to tell you something."

"What? Tell me already and give me the damn mirror."

"I need to tell you that there's hope for you, despite your injuries. See, there's a new, experimental procedure that, if it works, can make you relatively whole in a matter of a month, instead of years. It will be painful and require a number of unorthodox surgeries, but if you're strong, we can at least get you looking relatively normal in a very short amount of time."

"Fine, fine, it all sounds great, but I still don't know what's wrong with me. Now, give me that damn mirror, Doc, or I swear you're gonna regret it."

The doctor handed the mirror to him and took a few steps back. The patient was a big man and the police had said he had a record a mile long, everything from assault and battery to a suspect in a number of murders. He was a street thug, a man who would kill his mother for a dollar.

The mirror went up so that the patient could see his face, and the doctor swallowed the lump in his throat at the same time. It took less than a second for the screams to start, and as the patient got out of bed and began destroying the room after smashing the mirror, the doctor was already in the hallway and running for the nurses' desk while yelling, "Get the police here at once!"

That had been weeks ago, and after countless, experimental-yet-cutting-edge plastic surgeries in a very short time, Lenny the thug was replaced by a man named Puzzleface, who was brought into existence out of the necessity for revenge.

Revenge for what the Cowl had done to him.

Sure he'd been a petty thief who had graduated to assault and robbery, but that didn't give the Cowl the right to smash his face into an alley wall when he and a few buddies had tried to roll an old, rich married couple.

But none of that mattered now. His face might not have been what it once was but that was okay, for now, he was someone to be feared. One look at his face and the other guys he knew fell right in line, whether it was because of the perpetual scowl he always wore or because of the patchwork of flesh he now called his face; all that mattered to Lenny was that the men followed him absolutely.

Once the Cowl was killed and his revenge was complete, he could focus on more important things, such as growing his criminal empire across the city, and it looked like that was about to happen, as he'd seen the Cowl go down in the shelving unit collapse with his own eyes.

"Get in there, you guys," he snapped at his men, who had watched the LAW rocket in awe as it soared across the warehouse. "Find me the Cowl and make sure he's dead!"

"And if he's not?" a thug asked.

"Then finish him off."

As the shelving unit collapsed, the explosion only a few yards below the Cowl, he reacted instinctively. Shooting a rappel line, he swung away from the path of destruction. As smoke and fire billowed out across the warehouse, the Cowl was moving to a safer spot four aisles over.

Landing easily amongst the crates, he quickly dropped down to the floor and began circling back. Smoke was filling the air and a fire had broken out thanks to the detonation of the rocket. Thugs were moving towards the debris, heedless of the fire, knowing that if they didn't do as Puzzleface ordered, they would wish it was they who had been blown up in the explosion instead of the Cowl.

Moving swiftly through the warehouse, he pulled a 'rang with an explosive tip, and after stopping at the end of another aisle, he slowly stepped around it until he could see the thugs from behind as they began searching for him.

"Psst, hey, I'm over here," he said, and as the last thug in the group turned around to see who had spoken, the Cowl threw the 'rang at him, the tip of the 'rang sinking two inches into the thug's throat. The man would have been dead no matter what, as the steel tip severed his jugular and sliced his voice box in half, but the Cowl wanted to make an example of the guy to put the fear of God into the rest.

It did a good job at first.

When the explosive tip of the Cowlarang went off, the thug's head, along with a good portion of his chest, simply disappeared in a cloud of pink gore that sprayed the rest of the men.

Utter chaos took over as the remaining thugs tried to figure out what had just happened. There had been no gunshot; their friend's upper body had just blown up, as if by magic.

Pulling another 'rang, the Cowl threw that one as well, the steel tip of the weapon hitting a man in the lower thigh. Looking down, the thug's face took on a look of consternation, at least for the three seconds before the tip exploded and his leg was blown clear off his body. Screaming in agony, he fell to the floor, while staring down at his missing leg in horror; blood spurted like a geyser from the jagged stump. If a tourniquet wasn't applied immediately, the man would be dead in seconds.

The Cowl had another 'rang in hand, and was about to throw it, doing a hell of a job decimating the opposing ranks, when Puzzleface stepped out from behind where the shelving unit had collapsed, a massive automatic weapon in his hand.

"Say hello to Big Bertha, Cowl. Her bark is way worse than her bite," Puzzleface said with an evil grin across his scarred face.

The Cowl only had a brief glimpse of the weapon the crime boss held. It was a wheel gun with a circular cartridge holder, like a Tommy gun, and a leather sling to let the gunman support the weapon on his shoulder, as well as a bandolier that fed directly into the wheel. It was gloss black as well, with a glowing red tip that sent out a beam of red light that allowed the shooter to see exactly where his bullets would end up. From muzzle to grip it was a little over three feet long with a folding stock. A meaner firearm hadn't been thought up in quite a while. If the other thug's had been carrying one as well, the Cowl never would have stood a chance.

But only Puzzleface carried one, the gun made for him personally from his exact specifications.

The Cowl saw Puzzleface at the exact same moment the crime boss spotted him, and both fired at each other simultaneously; the Cowl throwing the 'rang, Puzzleface shooting the gun, which was set to semi-auto. Because of this, only one large caliber bullet was fired from the barrel, but it was more than enough to kill the Cowl.

But Fate stepped in as the 'rang flew in a perfect trajectory to hit the oncoming bullet. Six feet in front of the Cowl, the 'rang was detonated, the large bullet decimated so that only shrapnel from its casing struck the Cowl. Still, he was blown back from the shockwave, thrown to the floor where he tried to suck in air, the force of the explosion taking the breath right from his lungs.

"Don't just stand there, you idiots!" Puzzleface screamed. "Go get the bastard!" He shook his head in frustration. How many times did he have to tell his men to get the Cowl? Were they scared? Or just didn't have any initiative.

Lying on his back on the floor, the Cowl knew he was at a disadvantage. Pulling another 'rang, he threw it at the oncoming men. But his aim was off thanks to the wind being knocked out of him, and the weapon landed a few feet in front of the advancing men. Still, when the tip ignited, sending a small blast wave and spraying concrete from the devastated floor at them, the thugs had no choice but to fall back and take cover.

The Cowl used that time to get behind a stack of crates, where he then got to his knees and threw a few smoke pellets into the area between him and the thugs.

For the time being, he was safe from attack, the thugs taking stock of how to proceed next.

The Cowl shook off his reverie of how he'd ended up pinned down in the warehouse, Puzzleface's thugs itching to get at him, and the crime boss also wanting a piece of the Cowl's hide.

From where the Cowl was hidden behind the crates, he could see an attack would be imminent. Yells from one thug to another told him that he was surrounded, some of Puzzleface's men moving to cover the Cowl's back. He'd thrown two 'rangs with explosive tips at the men at his back, the resulting explosions keeping the men at bay.

But then he was out of 'rangs with exploding tips, and though he had other 'rangs, those were the only ones that could do enough damage to stop Puzzleface's men in their tracks.

At the end of the aisle, Puzzleface paced back and forth, ranting and raving, his large gun slung across his back. "How is that guy still alive? I can't believe that asshole's luck. He should be dead by now, for Pete's sake!"

"We'll get him, Boss, we have him surrounded," one of the thugs said.

Puzzleface stopped pacing and turned to face the man. Then he reached out and grabbed the thug by his shirt. "You better, Carlo, or else heads are gonna roll. You get me?"

"Sure, Boss, sure, I get ya. He's as good as dead, I promise."

Puzzleface held the thug for another heartbeat, then shoved the man away from him. Looking down the aisle, he saw where the Cowl had taken cover. He balled his hands into fists.

Soon.

Soon he would have his revenge.

Puzzleface didn't wait long. In reality he couldn't. He was too anxious to fulfill his promise to himself to kill the Cowl.

He waited for only ten minutes, and then with his men walking before him, they began moving down the aisle, firing their weapons to keep the Cowl on the offensive, while from the opposite side, the thugs there advanced as well.

Bullets struck the crates the Cowl was behind, splintering the wood and spilling the contents across the floor. Cupie dolls, thousands of them, had been taken to the warehouse from the seaport by customs to then be forgotten when the tariffs were never paid.

The dolls were shot to hell, faces blown off, little arms and legs severed at the torsos as round after round was poured into the spot where the Cowl was hidden. There was no return fire via Cowlarangs or smoke pellets, for the barrage was too much. If the Cowl so much as poked his head up, it would have been shot off.

Puzzleface did his own amount of damage to the Cowl's cover. The massive gun he carried firing again and again on full auto, shredding anything he aimed it at.

Finally, the first few thugs reached the end of the aisle, and as they turned to face the Cowl, they saw his black cape and began shooting at it. Hundreds of rounds of ammunition struck the cape, the material no match for such a complete onslaught of artillery.

The material was shredded, the bullets passing through it to what lay beneath.

The form under the cape shook and jiggled, as bullet after bullet was absorbed by it. The form fell over, slumping to the cement floor, and still the thugs kept firing. They knew how slippery the Cowl was and weren't going to stop until the body under the cape was nothing but shredded meat.

Puzzleface shoved a few men aside, and began firing with his massive gun at almost point blank range. The holes in the cape expanded from the large rounds, the form absorbing each bullet as if it was a sponge.

Eventually, Puzzleface stopped shooting and let out a yell for everyone to ceasefire. At first the gunfire continued but then it began to taper off. One thug wouldn't stop however, and with a manic look on his face, he repeatedly fired into the still form. Puzzleface screamed at the thug to stop, but the man was in a world of his own. Angry at being ignored, Puzzleface walked up behind the thug and shot him in the back of the head. The thug dropped to the floor, headless, and Puzzleface looked at the rest of his men and said, "I ask you; what does a guy have to do around here to be listened to? Tell me, did I overreact or what?" He locked eyes with the closest thug.

"No, Boss, you were right to do it. Jimmy was a moron, he shoulda listened to ya," the thug replied, the other men all nodding and grumbling their agreement.

"Exactly." Puzzleface turned so that he was facing the still form of the Cowl. "Now to see this jerk's dead eyes looking up at me. Man, I'm gonna savor this moment forever." He walked until he was standing over the Cowl's body, and with his right foot, he hooked it under the form and then shoved the body over, his eyes already going wide with the anticipation of seeing his enemy dead.

The body rolled over far too easily though, as if it was lighter than it should be, and Puzzleface's eyes went wide, but it wasn't with satisfaction, it was with something else entirely.

Confusion.

"What the he…" he started to say, but was cut short as a dark shape dropped down from the ceiling of the warehouse, landing right in the middle of the thugs. They thought he'd been surrounded, but they'd been thinking laterally. He was the Cowl; he always had 'up' as well when needing a direction to go.

Before even one thug could raise a weapon, the Cowl was on the attack, punching and kicking so fast his limbs were nothing but a blur. To make sure the men stayed down when he hit them, he wore a set of brass knuckles. Jaws were shattered and cheekbones demolished as blow after blow took down the thugs.

Some of the men, panicking, began to try and shoot the Cowl, but when they fired, he was already in another place, so the bullets would only shoot another thug.

"Stop firing, you fucking idiots! You're only hitting yourselves!" Puzzleface screamed to no avail.

The action was furious but actually very brief. In less than a minute every thug was down, either killed by friendly fire or wounded with a broken jaw or other such ailments that incapacitated them to the point they were no threat.

Puzzleface raised his massive gun, sighting on the Cowl as the dark form shifted and swirled around his men, but before he could squeeze the trigger, the Cowl threw a 'rang at him. The steel tip wasn't holding an explosive charge, but it was razor sharp, and the tip of the 'rang bit deep into the crime boss' right hand as he held the gun. The fingers spasmed, the act of squeezing the trigger now impossible. Needing his right hand to work the trigger as the left leveled the heavy weapon, there was no way he could fire the thing, so he threw it to the floor and pulled a pistol from within his suit with his left hand. "That won't stop me, Cowl. I can just as easily kill you with a regular gun than with Big Bertha." He began to shoot at the Cowl, who dodged from side to side, jumping and weaving, the bullets missing him by mere inches, and sometimes even less than that. Only one bullet scored a hit but it was a glancing blow, and though it slowed the Cowl down thanks to his previous injuries, he was still able to advance on Puzzleface, who when the gun clicked empty, threw the weapon at the Cowl out of desperation.

The Cowl avoided the thrown gun easily, then moved up to the crime boss and punched him in the jaw. Puzzleface went flying backwards, and as he landed on the floor, he began spitting teeth.

"You know, Puzzleface, Clownface shot one of his men at the bank for doing the exact same thing you killed that man for earlier when he wouldn't stop shooting. Maybe the two of you are more alike than you care to admit," the Cowl said.

"Me and that painted idiot are nothing alike!" Puzzleface replied. "And I heard you killed him—snapped his neck like a twig. At least, that's what the police autopsy said." He wiped fresh blood from his chin with the back of his hand. "So, is it true?"

"What if it is?"

Puzzleface shrugged. "Hey, it doesn't matter to me, but it's nice to know who I'm fighting. Good to know there's no line being drawn here. It's me kill you or you kill me, there's no middle ground." While he was talking, as if he was in a bar chatting with a friend, his left hand was reaching around to his back, where a knife was secreted. "You don't recognize me, do you?"

"Should I?"

"Yeah, you should." Puzzleface quickly explained how the Cowl had ruined his face by smashing it into a brick wall and about the experimental surgeries. "And this was the best they could do in the amount of time I gave the doctors. See, I wasn't going to wait around for a year or more. I needed to get back out on the streets and build an army so I could find you and enact my revenge by killing you."

"Oh really. And how's that working out for you?"

Puzzleface wrapped his hand around the hilt of the knife, as he slowly got to his feet. The Cowl was standing at ease and Puzzleface inwardly laughed. The fool thought he was helpless now that he was out of guns. How wrong the Cowl was.

The two men stood only a few feet apart.

"So what now?" the Cowl asked, knowing exactly what would happen. The Cowl would take the crime boss into custody and the police would find the man tied up in the warehouse, surrounded by dead bodies and devastation. The fires from the LAW rocket were still burning but weren't raging out of control yet. Smoke was filling the building, but with such high ceilings, the air was still breathable down on the floor, even when a person was standing.

"This is what," Puzzleface said, once more his voice staying calm, so that there was no sign of the attack until it came. He moved fast, faster than the Cowl would have expected, and the blade soared through the air, the crime boss holding the hilt tight as he charged at the Cowl.

Even with his reflexes, the Cowl was taken off guard, but he managed to recover in the nick of time. The blade struck dead left center of his chest, the force so powerful that the tip actually penetrated his Kevlar, though the blade was vastly slowed down. Still, a full inch slid into the flesh beneath his battle suit, the first inch of the knife sliding between two ribs and stopping centimeters from his heart. Only the Cowl's hands on Puzzleface's wrist prevented the blade from going deeper.

"You're gonna die now," Puzzleface hissed as he tried to push the knife deeper into the Cowl's chest.

The Cowl said nothing in reply, his concentration solely on keeping the blade from going into his heart. He swore if he focused hard enough, he could actually feel the tip of the blade caress his heart.

Puzzleface laughed as he began to overcome the Cowl's strength, his need for revenge fueling him to what he felt was glory; his payment was about to come due, in the form of the Cowl's life.

Sweat rolled down the Cowl's face from under his mask. His jaw taut, he closed his eyes and tuned out everything else: Puzzleface's laughter, the fires still burning, the cloying smoke that was now coming down from the ceiling to fill every space in the warehouse.

He turned it all off, his attention fully locked on the blade in his chest.

"What the fu… No, stop that," Puzzleface said as the Cowl began to get the upper hand. Ever so slowly, the blade was removed, until it parted from the tear it had created in the battle suit. Blood instantly squirted out of the tear, but after the initial second or two, the flow slowed to a more manageable level. If the Cowl could staunch the wound fast, he would have no problem surviving it.

Puzzleface's eyes were wide as he fought the Cowl for control of the knife. It was his knife, the one he was supposed to plunge into the Cowl's heart and end their little battle of wills. But Puzzleface quickly realized that though his face struck fear in the thugs of the city, and made them fall in line and work for him, to the Cowl, Puzzleface was just another criminal, albeit wearing a suit instead of some kind of colorful costume.

The Cowl managed to spin the knife around so that the tip was now aimed at Puzzleface's heart. "Surrender," was all he said.

"Never," Puzzleface whispered. "I won't stop till you're dead. I'll find out who you are under that mask and I'll kill anyone who you ever loved or knew. Family, friends, I'll bury them all before I come for you last, so that way you can know the pain and suffering you brought on all of them. But what I really want is for you to know the suffering I felt when you destroyed my face forever."

"Last chance," the Cowl said though gritted teeth.

"You won't kill me. I know all about you. You don't kill. Sure, you killed my men, but hey, they were trying to take you out, too, right? I bet Clownface was an accident. Am I right?" He peered into the Cowl's eyes. "Sure it was. I bet you were gonna take him in and the moron tried something." He shook his head, then lessened his grip on the hilt of the knife. "Nah, I'm not gonna fight ya anymore, Cowl. Take me to jail, and when I get out, I'm gonna start looking up those relatives of yours."

The Cowl felt the knife become more in his control, and the second he realized it, he plunged it into Puzzleface's chest, the blade slicing the left ventricle, the heart beginning to stop instantly.

"It's funny, Clownface said almost the exact same thing to me before I snapped his neck," the Cowl hissed.

Puzzleface had seconds to live, if that. The crime boss' face took on a look of pure amazement. "But I, but I…" he started but the Cowl cut him off.

"Yes, that's right. I killed you."

"But you can't kill me, you can't. You're not supposed to be a killer."

"You're thinking of the old Cowl. Thanks to criminals like you, I'm now just as much a killer as the rest of you." He sneered as Puzzleface spit blood, the man's bodily functions shutting down. "You and the rest of your kind have made me who I am now. I hope you're happy."

Puzzleface's mouth opened and closed, more blood seeping from the corners of his mouth. He tried to say something but it wouldn't come out. He spasmed once, more of a twitch really, then went limp.

The Cowl set the body down, then turned and walked away. He only stopped to retrieve his cape, which was now mostly in shreds thanks to the barrage of bullets it had been subjected to. As he pulled the cape to him and rolled it up into a ball, more than thirty bullet-riddled Cupie dolls fell to the floor. A piece of rappel line had been used to tie them together, but the line had been shot up as well so the dolls tumbled free. Still, the dolls tied together had made a hasty decoy before he'd sent a rappel line to the ceiling and waited to drop down in the midst of the thugs.

Wincing as he wrapped the cape up, he placed a hand to his chest and saw fresh blood. He knew he had to act fast to stop the bleeding, so going to one of the thugs, he grabbed the dead man's gun, popped out the magazine and took out a few bullets. He then quickly pried open the tips of the rounds with the edge of a Cowlarang before packing the powder into his wound. Taking a lighter from a pocket in his utility belt, he set the powder on fire. It ignited, hissing and smoking, a bright white light flashing out from his chest. The Cowl went to his knees, gasping from the pain, and he was scared that he was going to pass out. But then the fuzziness in his mind faded and he shook his head to clear it. His chest was on fire with pain but he was okay with it. The pain kept him awake, kept him focused.

The fires from the LAW rocket were still burning, so he went to a few wooden crates, and with the butt of the same dead thug's gun, he broke them open. More dolls spilled out and he gathered a few, stuck them into the fire by their heads, and when the cloth hair was good and burning, he began tossing them anywhere it looked like the fire would catch.

The warehouse had a lot of trash and debris, such as old shipping labels and newspapers, all piled in corners of the building. This was excellent kindling, and soon the fires were burning even hotter, and from there it would need no help consuming the warehouse and its contents.

With his chest in agony, the Cowl left the warehouse by a door, rather than from out through the roof, where he'd found a ventilation duct and used it as an egress upon first arriving.

As he climbed onto his motorcycle minutes later, something in the warehouse exploded, and dark black smoke began to pour out of anyplace the smoke could find. Soon the air was permeated with the odor of the burning building.

But below that, if someone knew the smell, recognizing it for what it was, there was the redolence of burning human flesh, as the bodies of the thugs and Puzzleface were burned to nothing but ash and brittle bones.

Gunning the engine of the black motorcycle, the Cowl drove away. But as he rode down the city streets, he looked at the sprawling metropolis in a new light.

In the future, when he battled evil, he wouldn't hold back for the sake of a moral code that had been shattered far too many times to be real. Looking back, he realized his morality had been foolish, a childish dream that didn't belong in the real world.

No, to stop evil in all its forms, there could be no line drawn in the sand, and that to do what was right, he needed to accept that the ends justified the means.

Clownface had been right when he'd given The Cowl a nickname.

Though the Cowl would always be a champion for the weak, and a savior for the innocent, he finally understood that his morality was foolish.

To keep them all safe he had to become what he swore never to be, but despite it all had become one anyway.

Yes, he would always be a hero.

But he would also be a *killer*.

VICTORY OF THE DEAD

ANTHONY GIANGREGORIO